ERIK VS. EVERYTHING

BY CHRISTINA USS

Clarion Books

An Imprint of HarperCollins*Publishers*

Library of Congress Cataloging-in-Publication Data is on file.
ISBN 978-0-06-329082-2

The text was set in Georgia.
Illustrations by Alan Brown
Cover and interior design by Catherine Kung
23 24 25 26 27   PC/CWR   10 9 8 7 6 5 4 3 2 1

First paperback edition, 2023

This book is for you, anytime you wish you could hide under a bed.

TABLE OF CONTENTS

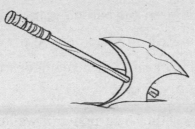

ONE

THE SHEEPFLATTENERS

Look backward to find the way forward.
— Sheepflattener Family Lore

Erik's heart hammered in his chest as though Thor himself were tunneling out of his rib cage. His mother sat next to him, reading a romance novel.

Erik whispered, "Please. Please don't make me go in there."

"What?" Mrs. Sheepflattener put a finger inside the book to mark her place and turned to Erik. "You'll need to speak up, dear, I can't understand a word you're saying," she said. Loudly. Loudly was the only way Mrs. Sheepflattener said anything.

The other children and parents glanced over. A dozen eyes focused on Erik. He had opened his mouth to try begging for mercy again when the door marked STUDIO #3 opened. It was too late.

A blond girl with a neat ponytail walked out. "Very good, Emma. Keep practicing those minor scales, now," said Mrs. Loathcraft, waving goodbye. She saw Erik cowering in his seat, and her face creased into a frown. "Erik," she said, as though his name had a funny taste. "You're next. Come in." She turned and disappeared into the room.

Erik didn't move. His insides prickled, and the hammering in his heart grew more insistent—*ka-thump! Ka-thump! KA-BLAM! KA-BLAM!* The veins in his ears throbbed. The arteries in his eyes pulsed. His whole body said NO.

Erik's mother clucked her tongue. She grabbed his arm and lifted him out of his seat. "Honestly, show your teacher some respect. Hupsy-daisy!" she said. In three steps, she dragged his entire body across the waiting room and propelled him into the studio. "Have fun!" The door shut behind him.

Forty-five minutes later, Erik's weekly piano lesson was over. It is safe to say that having fun as his mother had commanded was never an option.

~

After Erik and Mrs. Sheepflattener arrived home, Erik shuffled in from the garage and found his older sister Brunhilde had her battle-axe out and did not look pleased. Her twin, Allyson, was clutching a sweater to her chest and yelling, "I told you, this sweater is MINE. Yours is, like, gray! This one is SLATE!"

Brunhilde squinted at the sweater for a few seconds and shook her head. She started hefting her axe from hand to hand and growled, "Mine."

Erik knew better than to get in the middle of this. He stayed near the wall.

Allyson grabbed a vial of nail polish off the kitchen counter and said, "Don't wave that old axe at ME, sister. You come one step nearer, and I'll totally douse the sweater with this and neither of us can ever wear it again!" She started to untwist the cap, glaring at Brunhilde.

The axe-wielding twin rocked back on her heels,

assessing Allyson with clear blue eyes. "You would ruin it rather than let me claim it?" she asked.

Allyson snarled and nodded.

"Well played." Brunhilde put the axe down next to the pantry and tossed a blond braid over her shoulder. Their mother came into the room with bags of groceries from the car. "Mother, by Valhalla's rafters, I am hungry. My victory in the soccer scrimmage will be sung of for centuries to come. What is for dinner tonight?" Brunhilde had been speaking and acting this way ever since the last time Granny Vigdis had come to visit. After Granny announced that the teenager was the spitting image of some Viking-era relative known for her battle-planning skills, it was if she'd flicked some switch connecting Brunhilde with the Middle Ages. Erik might have been irritated by his sister's obsessive channeling of her ancestral Viking spirit if it hadn't suited her so perfectly well.

Their mother, ignoring the axe in the corner, started sorting groceries on the countertop. "Fish hunks, fish chunks, fish lumps, and mutton, dear," she said. "Both of you, start setting the table, please. We're eating early so Erik can make it to baseball practice. Erik, go find your uniform."

Allyson slipped the slate-gray sweater over her head and bounced over to the cupboard. Disagreements between the sisters were easily forgiven and forgotten, especially when Allyson ended up wearing the clothes she wanted to wear. "Your scrimmage actually was pretty songworthy, Bru. Did you hear the cheer I was working on with the squad? I was trying out rhyming *leap tackler* with *Sheepflattener*, although you're not, like, technically supposed to tackle anyone in soccer." The girls discussed tricky rhymes and why more sports need tackling while they got out the silverware and dishes.

Erik plodded upstairs to his small bedroom. He gathered himself on the threshold, took a flying leap, and landed on top of his bed. He jumped up and down three times as hard as he could, huffing, "Out! Out! Out!" He then flopped down flat on his stomach and peered into the dusty space below his quilt. If he saw any hint of a squirrel under there, he was ready to leap back out the door in three-quarters of a second—he'd clocked himself—but he saw nothing more than empty wood floorboards and his stack of comic books. As he saw every day. There had never yet been a squirrel under his bed, or any animal of any kind, for that matter. But every day was a new day, which was why he always came into his room the same way.

Satisfied it was safe, Erik slid to the floor and crawled under the low-hanging quilt. His bed was shoved up against two walls in the corner, plus he'd layered rocks and bricks to block off most of the rest of the space between the floor and the bed frame. There was only one opening big enough for a skinny nine-year-old to slither through.

His mom had been annoyed when he'd blocked it off, since she couldn't fit a broom under it, and insisted that Erik keep it clean himself. He didn't. He lay among the dust bunnies and Scooby-Doo comics with barely enough energy left to dread his upcoming baseball practice, falling into an uneasy doze until Brunhilde knocked on his door to announce dinner was on the table. He glumly changed into his uniform and went downstairs.

Thorfast Sheepflattener towered over the head of the table. His wife passed him a slab of bread, and he got busy slathering it with butter and honey. His father, Granddad Golveg, visiting for a month from Norway, sat to Thorfast's right with a bowl of mashed turnips. (Granny Vigdis had stayed home, saying she needed a month without her husband underfoot to do a really good spring cleaning.) Granddad was smiling to himself and sneaking bits of turnip to Spjut, the family's tiny terrier, whose name meant "spear."

"Spee-yoot, Spee-yoot, Spee-yoo-hoo-hoo-hoot," he murmured in a creaky singsong voice. "Even the littlest spear can slash." Spjut thumped his stubby black and white tail on the floor, clearly enjoying this acknowledgment of his spearlike doggy toughness as much as he enjoyed the turnip morsels.

Erik sat down and pushed his mutton around his plate. He nibbled a bite of bread. His stomach swayed like a hammock in anticipation of baseball practice. Maybe if he ate less than normal, he wouldn't throw up quite so much this time when he went up to bat.

"How was work today, Dad? Any good corporate raiding going on?" asked Allyson, heaping her plate with meat and fish.

Their father chewed, honey leaving a glistening trail on his beard. He grunted twice, wiped his chin with the back of his hand, and gestured for the fish platter.

Allyson waited a moment to see if her father had anything to add. "Cool," she said. Thorfast Sheepflattener's children knew he was a man of few words, and even fewer grunts.

Erik's mother took hold of the conversation and announced, "Fafner looks ready to be brought to auction." She raised draft horses on their large property and sold them to farms around New England. "That colt is almost as big as his sire now. You girls have really helped me with him, so I've decided that you'll each get a portion of his sale price for your own use." Allyson's smile dimpled her cheeks. Brunhilde nodded gravely. "Erik, now that you're nine, you can start helping with the horses too."

"Do I have to?" he said.

The rest of the family looked at him, mild puzzlement on every face. Even Spjut stopped gnawing on a mutton bone and looked up. Erik dropped his eyes. He wasn't sure why so many meals with his family ended up with him getting these kinds of looks.

"Well, no, dear," his mother said, "you don't have to. I thought you'd want to. Working with horses is such a joy, and what child doesn't want some money of their own?"

He stared down at his plate. "Can I be excused?"

Erik's mom shrugged, and the rest of the family went back to eating. "Fine. Clear your place and get your gear. We leave in fifteen minutes," she said.

After setting his plate in the sink, Erik went to the coat closet to find his baseball mitt. It wasn't there, so he checked the weapons closet. He finally found it buried underneath his mother's daggers, his father's club, Spjut's armor, and Allyson's pompoms. He dug it out and sat back, woozy. If only he could be preparing to stay home and read comic books in his room instead of this. That one bread nibble was turning his stomach from a swaying hammock into a rocking swing set. He wondered if he'd be seeing the bread again soon, maybe next to home plate.

Trying to let his innards settle down, he leaned against the wall and looked up at the family portraits hanging across from him. Anyone could see the family resemblance between his muscular, corn-blond twin sisters and the relatives glaring down from the photos above. Erik, not so much. He sometimes doubted any muscles grew between his skin and bones, and his shaggy hair was so much blonder than anyone else's in the family, it was almost white. He thought he more closely resembled the frantically burrowing albino mice at the pet store than anyone in the Sheepflattener clan.

His eyes slid to the honored photo of the family artifacts: a spear, a ladle, a fragment of a drinking horn, a fish-shaped iron rivet in a bit of boat timber, and an axe inscribed with the Sheepflattener name and a rune loosely translated as "Not to Be Trifled With." Every Sheepflattener kid knew the story. The artifacts had been discovered on the Sheepflattener family farm in Norway near the turn of the twentieth century. They'd been verified by university scholars as genuine Viking relics, so the family had gone gaga over collecting all possible evidence and stories directly linking them to those ferocious seagoing warriors of old. It turned out there were records of the Sheepflatteners having lived and adventured all over Scandinavia, from Norway to Sweden, Denmark, and Iceland.

The family had amassed quite a hoard of interesting historical information about the Sheepflattener clan when tragedy struck: everyone got hit with the rare but deadly lung-tooth plague. They were too sick to work, so they lost the farm. However, instead of giving up and dying dreadfully as one might have expected, they'd decided to try using some of their ancestors' old habits in order to stand up to the disease invading their bodies and turn their luck around. After all, the Sheepflattener Vikings had evidently survived and shown the world they were Not to Be Trifled With for more than a thousand years. Perhaps by looking backward, the family might find a path forward through their current misfortunes.

The stricken Sheepflatteners learned to read runes and called upon the Norse gods to look upon them with favor. They scoured their historical documents for the foods and recipes that had sustained their ancestors. (This turned out to be mostly fish and turnip stew.) They gave each other tattoos and stopped cutting their hair, believing this might imbue them with extra strength. To make money, they began handcrafting axes, spears, ladles, drinking horns, and fish-shaped iron rivets. And, by Fricka's socks, their plan worked. The plague fizzled out. They sold their handmade goods for tidy sums to tourists and reclaimed the farm, plus extra land. The young adult Sheepflatteners looked so great with their new beards and long braids that members of well-to-do families came to beg for their hands in marriage.

Those lucky Sheepflatteners vowed to never forget the power of their heritage and began organizing advice on how to live for all future Sheepflattener generations. Originally labeled *Hvordan Vi Gjør Ting* (How We Do Things), the family now called this collection of wisdom the Lore.

Each generation continued to add modern stories of how leaning on the Lore had gotten them out of tough spots: illness, poverty, hair loss — you name it, some branch of the family had a story about how getting their Viking on had helped them. An enterprising cousin had scanned all the old parchment and notebooks and uploaded the Lore, along with the English translation, to his website so any family member could easily access it.

Erik's family had downloaded and printed multiple copies. Brunhilde enthusiastically studied the Lore's instructions about weapons handling, and both sisters swore the Lore's proverbs helped them get through algebra class. Their mom said she'd added notes about how the Lore had eased her and Thorfast's adjustment to life in Connecticut after moving from Norway, plus how it had been the cure for everything after the twin girls were born prematurely. As far as Erik could tell, this family wisdom focused mostly on fishing and fighting. He liked the Lore's advice about calling upon the old gods when in peril, even though it rarely seemed to work.

Eyeing the clock ticking ever closer to baseball time, Erik decided it couldn't hurt to give the gods a try. He murmured, "Hail, Odin, Fricka, Thor, Loki, and everyone else. Erik Sheepflattener here. If any of you aren't too busy, please do something to cancel my baseball game. Maybe a thunderstorm? Or turn all the baseballs and bats into, I don't know, worms or something? Thanks in advance."

No Norse deity he knew of was likely to approve of such a pathetic request from a supposed Viking descendant. Erik knew that with his DNA, he ought to be a snarling, furry beast of a boy. He was, most assuredly, not. Even though no one else in his family seemed to know the meaning of the word *fear*, Erik knew all about it. Fear shook his insides when he got on the bus, at school, during sports practices and piano lessons, and the one time his mother dragged him to a sew-your-own-stuffed-animal day at the local craft shop, he had begun sobbing and sweating so hard she took him to the doctor's office, believing him to have the flu.

He sat up a little straighter, scanning the photos for any family members who weren't scowling at the camera as though they would overpower anything that came their way. He examined a photo of his Miami cousins flaunting skimpy swimwear. Nope. Even his bikinied cousins looked like they could defend Miami Beach from sea monsters with a warship they'd constructed themselves out of palm trees.

His gaze landed on a recent photo of Granny Vigdis, and his stomach lurched. She proudly displayed her wrinkled rune tattoo, TROUNCE. Part of the Lore stated that adults in the Sheepflattener family each had an Old Norse rune, an ancient symbol, tattooed on their inner arms. Choosing your rune was part of a coming-of-age ceremony, and it served as your motto for life. His father's was PRIDE. Erik thought his mother's rune tattoo should have been HORSE, or maybe LOUD, but it was the symbol for FAMILY.

The rune-tattoo tradition seemed pretty iffy to Erik, since no historical proof confirmed it, but he guessed if you did something long enough and insisted that it was part of your family heritage long enough, it became so. He rubbed his bony arms, thinking about his own tattoo, which he would never get because even the idea of having ink pounded into his skin made him grit his teeth so hard he thought his upper and lower molars might fuse together. But if his family tied him down and insisted he pick something, he'd probably choose a rune that said AVOID STUFF. Or maybe just the word NO.

"Erik!" his mother yelled. "Time to g—" Mrs. Sheepflattener was drowned out by a thunderous *BOOM,* followed by the wet whoosh of a sudden downpour.

Just in case this was no coincidence, he bobbed his head to thank Thor. A lot of Ridgewell nine-year-olds would be disappointed this evening, but not Erik Sheepflattener. He stopped contemplating his family's heritage and tossed his mitt back in the closet. He let go of his dread over heaving his guts out at baseball and headed upstairs to spend some time with his dread over going to school tomorrow.

TWO

THE ONLY THING WE HAVE TO FEAR

One can sew wings to a goat, but
that doesn't make it an eagle.
— The Lore

E rik's prickly feeling of dread kept him company through the night and during his ride on the school bus to Ridgewell Lower Elementary the next morning. The dread pricks mellowed out into a low feeling of nausea once he was sitting at his desk.

After some trial and error, Erik had found the best ways to avoid calling attention to himself in Mr. Sullivan's fourth-grade classroom were to turn in work that was good enough but not so good the teacher might want him to share it with the class, and to hunch ultra-low in his chair whenever things got too hairy. After a dozen or so incidents where Erik scrunched himself up small when asked to participate in class discussions, Mr. Sullivan had let him be. There were plenty of other kids who waved their hands to be called upon, plus other kids who were squirmy and distracted, so Mr. Sullivan had his hands full without having to focus on one slouchy boy.

Mr. Sullivan had begun a social studies unit about the US presidents earlier in the week. He wrote the name Franklin Delano Roosevelt on the board. "FDR was the first and last American president elected to four terms. One of his most famous quotes was 'The only thing we have to fear is fear itself,'" he said.

Erik started. "That's not true," he said, the words jumping out of his mouth.

Mr. Sullivan's eyebrows rose. "Sorry, was that you, Erik? Did you have . . . something to say?"

Erik felt more words bubbling up. His mouth seemed to have a mind of its own. "There's lots of other things to fear. Getting hurt? Feeling stupid?" The words came faster now, and louder. "School buses. Running squir-rels. Crouching squirrels. Squirrels in trees. Squirrels under beds. Baseball. Football. Basketball. Dodgeball. Kickball. Volleyball. Every kind of ball. Having things thrown at you. Having things yelled at you. Having peo-ple stare at you."

The other kids were staring at him.

His innards turned hard and sharp, and his tongue suddenly felt two sizes too large. At least with this big, unwieldy slab of tongue to deal with, his traitorous mouth gave up and stopped talking. He clamped his lips shut and slid way, way down; this time he went com-pletely off of his chair and ended up tucked underneath his desk.

As soon as he slid out of view, the other kids lost interest and went back to hand raising and squirming. They were accustomed to Erik disappearing under stuff. Most of his classmates had known him since kinder-garten, when they'd drawn him in-class birthday cards featuring pictures of his desk with his legs sticking out from underneath it. (He had a couple of friends who liked to hang out and read comic books and graphic novels like he did, and he appreciated that they never made a big deal about his tendency to hide under furniture.) Mr. Sullivan, who had been staring at Erik too, gave his head a shake and went on to explain President Roosevelt's handling of World War II.

Time passed ever so slowly under Erik's desk until the bell rang for the end of the day.

Spjut was waiting when the school bus pulled up into the Sheepflatteners' neighborhood. He sniffed each child as they disembarked and gave most of them a tail wag. Erik was the last one off. The boy trudged toward his front yard. The little dog followed at his heels until the neighbors' enormous German shepherd strutted by. Spjut barked out a challenge and chased the much bigger dog down the street. Spjut Sheepflattener didn't appear to know the meaning of the words *fear* or *much bigger dog.* Despite weighing no more than a scrawny rabbit, he acted like he was the most intimidating animal in town.

Spjut dashed back in time to follow Erik through their front door. Erik snuck past his mother sitting at the kitchen table and headed up the stairs. The terrier followed, his tiny toenails clicking on the wooden stair risers, and reached the top to watch Erik do his bed-jumping, squirrel-repelling routine. Spjut settled down with a fragrant doggy sigh on Erik's rug, ready for a nice nap while Erik did whatever it was he liked to do under that bed every afternoon.

Erik blew a fluff of dust out of his way and rolled over on his back to think about school. How could he AVOID another scene like that? He'd been toying with the idea of making his own personalized list of Lore-like survival tips, starting with *He who can avoid stuff will not be destroyed by stuff.* Maybe he could come up with a saying to remind himself to keep quiet.

"Keep one's lips stuck together except when eating," he said out loud. Granddad's deer-hide slippers appeared below the quilt. His wrinkled face appeared next, upside down.

"Hi, Granddad," Erik said. He wondered whether his grandfather had heard what he'd said.

Granddad Golveg gave him a wave, and Erik caught a glimpse of his faded tattoo (the symbol for TURNIP).

"Better to speak too little than too much," the old

man said, quoting a translation of Erik's father's favorite bit of the Lore. Wisdom delivered, he straightened up and shuffled away, humming.

Erik stretched his legs toward the wall and picked up a graphic novel about aliens. He wasn't moving from this spot until he absolutely had to. When he'd crept past his mom, he had seen the Ridgewell Recreation catalog open on the kitchen table in front of her, the frightening words **Youth Lacrosse** and **Introduction to Drama** and **African Drumming Circle** in bold on the page. Although he had pleaded with her before every activity as though he were being sent to fight in a hopeless battle, never to return, their conversation was always the same:

"Mom, no," he had said, watching Cub Scouts setting up painted wooden cars on the Pinewood Derby track.

"Mom, no," he had said, grabbing the doorjamb to resist being pushed inside the local tae kwon do dojo.

"Mom, noooooooo!" he had howled, his mother hauling him to junior swim team tryouts and plopping him into the shallow end.

"Erik, yes," she said back. Occasionally, she'd add

some nugget of child-raising wisdom, like "One must howl with the wolves one is among," or "Children must stay busy," and would hear no more on the subject.

Erik listened in despair to the scratching of his mom's pen as she filled out his contact information for yet another thing he didn't want to do. The scratching was interrupted when the phone rang. Erik yelled, "Gaaah!" like he always did when the phone rang. His yelp petered out into a groan. He'd already failed at keeping his lips stuck together.

Mrs. Sheepflattener didn't react to the yelp. No one in the family ever did. Erik yelling "gaaah!" after the phone rang was as unsurprising as a light coming on after you flipped the switch.

"Bjorn, how are you?" she said to the caller. Uncle Bjorn was Erik's father's brother. "How are Hilda and the babies? And how are Ragnar and Hrolf enjoying being big brothers to so many?" Aunt Hilda had given birth to triplets, two boys and a girl, shortly after Christmas. "Oh? Mmm-hmmm. I understand. Yes . . . yes . . . well, of course, we'd be happy to help." She shifted some papers around. "Uh-huh, school is done by then. Certainly, Erik would be thrilled to see his cousins. What boy wouldn't be?"

Erik's heart thumped. He was pretty sure he and his mother didn't agree on the meaning of the word *thrilled*.

"He'll be there. Give all the children and Hilda a hug from all of us. Goodbye!" Mrs. Sheepflattener hung up the phone and clapped her hands together. "Erik, downstairs please, I have news! Girls, you too!"

Erik and his sisters obeyed.

"Uncle Bjorn called to say the triplets are growing beautifully, hitting milestones faster than they expected. He and Aunt Hilda can already tell they're going to have their hands full by the time the little ones start to crawl this summer. Your uncle asked if any of the cousins could come up and lend a hand around the house. I told them Erik could."

Erik's jaw dropped. "Me?" he squeaked. The Minnesota Sheepflatteners had leaned on the Lore with a vengeance by raising and hunting their own food after his aunt and uncle both lost their jobs. Erik couldn't imagine how he could be of any help.

"Of course you. Allyson has cheer camp, and Brunhilde is planning on lifeguard training this summer," his mother said. "Babies are straightforward, dear, it won't be hard to figure out. Rock them, feed them, don't let badgers eat them, it's plain and simple. And family always looks after family! Speaking of looking after things, I need the three of you to clean up the dining room before dinnertime." She walked over to the back of the pantry door where the cleaning supplies hung and grabbed the straw broom. "I don't want any axe-grinding stones in the way when your father gets home."

Mrs. Sheepflattener shoved the broom into Erik's hands, and he dragged himself after his sisters. *Just when you think the worst thing you have to fear is the Recreation catalog, along come triplets learning to crawl.* Erik felt like he'd been triple-punched in the stomach. *Cousins*—pow! *Babies*—pow! *A summer hundreds of miles away from his own bed*—ka-pow!

Allyson bounced from the kitchen into the dining room and started collecting the loose bits of chain she'd been hammering into a stylish yarn-and-chain-mail scarf. Brunhilde stomped over to gather her axe-cleaning tools.

It was easy to tell which girl had been working on which side of the room. Erik believed his twin sisters must have agreed at birth that being born on the same day didn't mean they were the same. One sister got her fashion hints from teen magazines; the other from centuries-old war poems. Brunhilde took great pride in sharing her name with a mythic Valkyrie maiden; Allyson had insisted since preschool that everyone call her something "more Connecticutty," since her given name, Blóðughadda, proved impossible for any classmates to pronounce. Neither twin was old enough to have a rune tattoo yet, but like most Sheepflattener teenagers, they often copied different symbols on their arms to try them out. Today, Allyson's rune, sketched in strawberry-scented highlighter, said FUN. Brunhilde's own charcoal-traced tattoo was the same one she'd been choosing for months: CONQUER.

Erik started to sweep in twitchy bursts, poofing up a cloud of pink yarn clippings mixed with gray stone dust. As the pink and gray flotsam settled back down, he sneezed and leaned weakly on the broom, thinking that he'd probably end up having to share a bedroom in Minnesota with his boy cousins. What would his borrowed bed look like? Would it be close enough to the doorway that he could do anti-squirrel inspections with one leap? Would it have any space under it at all, or would it be crammed full of moose hides and war bows with no room for a boy to hide?

~

The room got cleaned, the table was set, and dinner was served when Thorfast walked in the door. He greeted them all with a fond grunt, and the whole family settled in to eat. Allyson talked about a school project to collect clothes for the homeless, and Mrs. Sheepflattener reminisced about when each of the kids was an infant and how much work new babies can be.

Brunhilde was quiet throughout the meal. Eventually, she put down her fork. "Mother," she said in her monotone voice.

"Yes, my iron flower?" Mrs. Sheepflattener said.

"Does Cousin Ragnar still practice boxing?" Brunhilde asked.

"Mmmm, I am pretty sure he does. He won that state championship for his weight class last year. My, how he likes hitting things. Every time he gets in the ring, someone learns the fists of Vikings are not to be trifled with!" Mrs. Sheepflattener said. Erik shivered. Ragnar was his oldest Minnesota cousin and always wanted to play games that involved smashing something.

Brunhilde swallowed and frowned. "You know the school still won't let me in the boxing ring at all. Not since I punched right through the punching bag and my glove came out the other side." She picked up a hunk of halibut from her plate and squeezed it until it dripped grayish juice. "Does Ragnar still have that throwing axe? And is Hrolf learning wrestling? Mother, may I accompany Erik in visiting the cousins? Perhaps they will train with me. It is difficult to find anyone strong and quick enough out here to fight with," she said. "I am a warrior in here" — she thumped her chest with a fist wet with halibut juice — "but I need more skills to be a warrior out in the world. Visiting the cousins might help."

"I hear you, dear," their mother said, refilling her

own plate. "Granny Vigdis always said you naturally take after our most combat-hungry ancestors. Letting you visit the cousins sounds fine to me. I'll call your uncle back after dinner and see what he has to say, but I imagine he'll be delighted to have you. You can help Erik with the babies!" she said.

Brunhilde grunted in satisfaction, and their father grunted in agreement. Erik looked at his sister, with her thick blond braids and sharp, serious face. Was having her along on the trip going to make it more or less terrifying? The last time the cousins got together, Brunhilde and Ragnar organized an offensive against a flock of geese that kept pooping on the school playground. Erik had never seen so many feathers.

He got lost in his imagination for a while, picturing Brunhilde and Cousin Ragnar inventing a combination of axe-fighting and boxing, or wrestling with wild animals, or designing plans to wage war on the local townsfolk. It seemed unlikely that his sister joining him was going to make the whole experience any calmer.

It was going to be a long summer.

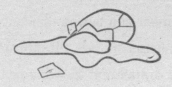

THREE

THE MINNESOTA VIKINGS

*You needn't swim faster than the shark, only
faster than the swimmer next to you.*
— The Lore

B runhilde clomped into Erik's room and dropped a pair of boxing gloves into his suitcase. "No more room in mine. You take these." She clomped back out.

The suitcase his mother had set out for him at the end of his bed was nearly full. He tried not to look at the bundle of his soft, defenseless shirts, pants, and underwear now wrinkled under Brunhilde's boxing gloves. In an hour, he'd have to zip that thing closed and drag it to the airport for his flight to Minnesota. The weeks since the phone call from Uncle Bjorn sealing his doom had slipped horribly past like rattlesnakes racing down a greased hill. He tried to be glad that he didn't have to show up for piano lessons for the five weeks they'd be gone, but it was a small comfort.

Erik folded his hands and tried petitioning Thor to whip up an airport-closing hurricane, aware that it would only delay things. He knew not even the old gods could make a hurricane last the entire summer.

It appeared Thor knew it too, because the dreamy blue June sky hosted the friendliest and puffiest hurricane-free clouds.

"A perfect day for flying!" his mother said several times on the way to the airport. Erik wondered if maybe she'd asked the gods for good weather before he'd asked for bad. It took hardly any time at all before he was clasping his boarding pass to Minneapolis/Saint Paul at the back of the security check line. Mom hugged him, and Brunhilde and his dad exchanged a couple of solemn grunts.

Allyson ruffled Erik's hair. "Have fun, Erik," she said. Then she gave Brunhilde an enthusiastic squeeze. "I'll,

31

like, miss you, sister. But any clothes you left behind are fair game for me to borrow, right?"

"No," said Brunhilde.

"Your mouth says no, but your unprotected closet says yes!" Allyson sang out.

Brunhilde responded, "My mouth and my closet both say no. Is that not clear? Do I need to make it clearer in a way you will not forget all summer?"

"No time for that now, girls!" Mrs. Sheepflattener admonished. "They're calling Brunhilde and Erik's boarding group. Now, Erik, do your best. I want to hear nothing from Hilda but how much you helped her with those babies, do you understand?"

He nodded stiffly, wondering if his fear of flying was about to dislodge his dread of visiting the cousins. Nope, he realized while hauling his suitcase up the jetway behind Brunhilde. His insides made room for them both.

~

After enduring a three-hour flight and one-hour bus ride, Erik and Brunhilde arrived at their uncle and aunt's house and were immediately enveloped by a passel of back thumps and roared greetings. Erik was planning on scoping out the bed situation, but his Aunt Hilda insisted she'd take care of the unpacking while the rest of the family brought him and Brunhilde out for some fresh air.

Aunt Hilda handed Uncle Bjorn a picnic basket that smelled of fish, instructing her husband, "You take your niece and nephew out to the lake, give them a chance to shake the dust of travel off themselves." She added, "And take the triplets too, they could use an airing out." His cousins bustled out the door, and Erik had no choice but to follow.

After the meal of fish cakes had been eaten, Erik hung back near the picnic blanket while eight-year-old Hrolf and fourteen-year-old Ragnar waded in the water and Brunhilde set up a ring of stones to make a fire pit. The triplet babies, Sven, Siegmund, and tiny Sally, were bundled up under animal pelts in their stroller, gazing around themselves as if they owned the woods and the lake and found them good.

Other than their small size, Erik found it hard to believe the triplets were only six months old. At this age, average babies might be trying to master sitting up. Hrolf had told him on the walk over to the lake that triplet babies are born tougher than average. After nine months of whacking into each other in their mother's womb before being born, even non-Viking triplets have better muscle control than other newborns. Assuming all babies were sort of hopelessly blobby and soft, Erik had been unprepared for the triplets' alert eyes and grasping hands. They seemed less like infants to him and more like miniature animals born ready to hunt.

"C'mon, Erik lad, get out there." Uncle Bjorn pointed at the lake.

"No, thanks," Erik said in a small voice. He didn't expect it to work any better on Uncle Bjorn than it did on his mother. He was right.

"You must not have heard me, lad. Get on out there! The fish won't catch themselves, you know," Uncle Bjorn said.

Erik looked out at the choppy, dark surface of the lake. It offered no hint of what might be prowling its depths. Young Hrolf ducked his head under the water to search for likely catfish hidey-holes.

Erik made no move to do anything. Uncle Bjorn looked flummoxed. "What are you waiting for?"

"I can't. I'm scared," Erik said in an even smaller voice.

"Scay-yerd?" His uncle rolled the word around in his mouth and munched his beard a bit. English was Bjorn's second language, and his grasp of words he never used could be a little shaky. "What's that mean, exactly?"

"You know, it's a feeling — kind of a poking, yawning feeling in your insides? When you have a fear that something bad is going to happen to you, or that you're going to get hurt? Or have to fight?" Erik said.

Uncle Bjorn chuckled. "Nephew, don't you know yet that having to fight is one of the best feelings in the world? We'll make sure you get plenty of chances to learn about that, by Valhalla!" He clapped Erik on the shoulder. Uncle Bjorn's rune tattoo was his own name, BJORN, Old Norse for *bear*.

"Fish on!" Hrolf emerged from under the water and waved his arm proudly. Well, he waved some of his arm proudly. The part from his elbow to his fingertips was covered in a whiskery two-pound catfish that had apparently swallowed Hrolf's hand. Erik stared in horrified fascination. Under the catfish's dangling whiskers, he could see his cousin had drawn a rough rune sketch on his forearm. It said EAT.

"Good job, son," yelled his father. "Bring it over!" Uncle Bjorn turned to Erik. "Well, if fishing isn't what you like, might as well help your sister build that fire." Erik looked over at Brunhilde. She was breaking sticks over her knee to fit them into the circle of stones. She found a smoothish one with a point and showed it to Sally, pretending to do a bit of sword-fighting with it. Sally reached for it and made a tiny grumbling noise. Brunhilde booped her nose with one finger.

Hrolf came splashing out of the water. While his name meant "wolf" in Old Norse, sturdy Hrolf was more stump-shaped than wolfish. He hustled over so his father could yank the catfish off of him and begin gutting it. Erik backed up a couple of steps to move out of their way, bumping into Cousin Ragnar.

Ragnar grabbed Erik's arm. "Erik, there's a pike over there almost as big as you are," he said. "Come see!"

"No, no, really, Ragnar, but thanks anyway—" Erik began to say, but was yanked back toward the lake's edge. He tried digging his sneakers into the sand to slow Ragnar down, but his older cousin didn't seem to notice. A couple of months younger than Brunhilde and Allyson, Ragnar was already as tall as an adult and had tufts of hair beginning to sprout across his body. His rune tattoo sketch was SMASH.

"This old pike, we see him sometimes, he looks really delicious. Mean as a wolverine, too. He has teeth growing out of his teeth," Ragnar said with admiration. They reached the edge of the water, and Ragnar kept dragging, pulling Erik right into the lake up to his thighs near an area grown thick with reeds. "This is where we saw him. Oh, yeah! Look, there he is now!" And Ragnar, probably assuming any boy would love to catch a fish with his face, grabbed Erik by the back of his jacket and shoved his head toward the water.

By golly, Ragnar was right. That was one large, tooth-covered fish. Erik and the pike regarded each other for a moment. The yellow-green fish's attention fell on Erik's windbreaker zipper. It considered the glitter of the shiny steel zipper pull, then opened its mouth, flipped its tail, and lunged up to snag the zipper pull with one saw-edged fang. Erik leapt backwards, but the pike held on to that tasty zipper. Its fishy lips flapped on his canvas coat looking for a better grip. Erik stumbled toward the shore while the pike's wet body thrashed back and forth against his torso.

Erik howled, "BABABADALGHARAGHTAKAMMI-NARRONNKONNBRONNTONNERRONNTUONNT-HUNNTROVARRHOUNAWNSKAWNTOOHOOHOO-RDENENTHURNUKAAAAAAARGGGGGGG-NOOOOOOOOOOAAAAAAAAAAAAAAW-WWWWWWWWHHHHHHHHHHHHH-HHUUUUUUUUUUUUUUUUUUUU-NOOOOOOOOOOOOOOOOOOOOOOOBAD-FISHBADFISHBADFISHAAAAAAUUUUUU UUUUUUUUUUUUUUUURRRRRRRRR RRRRGGGGUGUGGUGUGUGGGUGUGAAA-AAAAAAAAAAAAAAAAAAAAAAAAA!" so loudly that the oak trees shook and geese took off for the south three months ahead of schedule. He flailed, trying to grab a fin or flipper and pull the behemoth off himself, but the pike's scales were slippery and he couldn't get a grip.

Ragnar whooped in excitement, "Fish on!" He took a boxing stance and started punching at the fish's gills. It was still whipping around, so Ragnar accidentally landed a hairy-knuckled blow on Erik's stomach, winding him and knocking him over onto the sandy shore. (At least that paused the screaming.) Hrolf snatched a stick from the fire pit for fish flogging. Brunhilde wheeled over the triplets' stroller so they wouldn't miss out.

Uncle Bjorn looked on in satisfaction. "That beast must weigh as much as Erik does. Told him we'd show him the joys of having to fight."

Brunhilde picked up a large branch and was about to join the fray when she stopped and cocked her head, studying her brother's face. He still hadn't gotten his wind back and was desperately trying to suck in some air. The fish lashed its long body back and forth, yanking Erik's chest up and slamming it back down with every lunge. Erik looked up at her, tears running from the corners of his eyes, and mouthed, *Don't let me die like this.*

Brunhilde ran to Erik's head until she was facing the pike head-on, took aim, and shoved her branch into the pike's mouth as far as she could. She shouted with effort and heaved the fish off her brother. It launched up into the air like a pole vaulter, flipping over several times and landing with a massive splash back in the water. Apparently no worse for the wear, it flapped its tail once against the surface of the lake and was gone.

The Minnesota kids moaned at having lost such a tasty morsel.

"Ah well, that pike's a tough bugger. He lives to fight us again," Uncle Bjorn said. "Plenty more fish in the lake, children, plenty more. What did you think of that, then, Erik?" he asked.

Erik opened his mouth and replied, "AAAAAAAAA AAAAARRRRRWHHHYYYYYYYAAAAAAAAAAAA AAAAFANGSFANGSFANGSFISHFANGSTHOUGHTI-WASGONNADIEAAAAAAAAAAAAAAAAAAAAAA ARGHUUUUUUUUUUUUUUUPERKODHUSKURUN-

BARGGRUAUYAGOKGORLAYORGROMGREMMITG-
HUNDHURTHRUMATHUNARADIDILLIFAITITILL-
IBUMULLUNUKKUNUNUUUUUUUUUUUUUUUU
UUUUUURRRRRRRRRRRRRRRRRRRRRRRRRRR
RRRGGGGGGGGGGGGGGGGGGGGGGGGGHHHHHH-
HHHHHHHHHAAAAAAAAAAAAAAAAAAAAAAAA
AAAAAHH!" The magnificent scream echoed over the
water, startling a family of quail near the edge of the
woods.

Brunhilde dropped her branch and ripped off
one sleeve of her shirt. "I'll stop the bleeding," she
announced, and knelt next to her brother, unzipping his
windbreaker while he continued shrieking. She checked
for wounds on his body, arms, and legs. She peeled back
his eyelids and looked into both of his eyes. His shrieks
trailed off into whimpers.

She leaned back. "No blood," she murmured. "Yet
you screamed like you were at death's door."

"I was," Erik managed in a hoarse whisper.

Everyone else waded back into the lake, but she
stayed kneeling at her brother's side, rubbing her chin.
Erik lay limply on the damp ground, covered in fish

mucus, and wondered how much more of this summer "vacation" he could take.

~

The family arrived home later bearing fish for Aunt Hilda to salt and store in the larder. "Well done, children," she commended them. "Did the triplets try their hands at catching any this time around?"

Young Hrolf hooted. "I used Sven as bait for the biggest one we caught, and he did a great job luring it in to shore!" He held his baby brother up in the air with a grin, as if dangling Sven's chubby little legs in front of a twelve-pound largemouth bass was the best way to babysit Viking infants. Perhaps it was, because his mother hugged them both in delight.

Erik sat down at the kitchen table and laid his cheek on his folded arms.

Brunhilde asked Aunt Hilda for a bowl of dried oatmeal, maple syrup, and milk. Instead of eating it herself, she plunked it in front of Erik with a spoon. Surprised, he glanced up.

Brunhilde sat down across from him, her forehead furrowed. "You yelled more loudly than I think you have ever yelled in your life. Even louder than at sew-your-own-stuffed-animal day. You were scared of the pike at the lake," she said. "That is why you were screaming, not because you were hurt, right?"

"Yes," he answered. "I mean, that was crazy! I think anyone would have been scared of that fish eating them alive!"

Brunhilde lowered her eyebrows even further, studying Erik like he was an important message written in a foreign tongue.

"I'm scared of a lot of things," Erik continued. The intense way his sister was staring at him made him keep talking. He stirred his spoon in the oats. "There's so much to be scared of, at home, at school, out here. I wish . . . I wish . . . I don't even know what I wish."

"Is that what makes you spend so much time under your bed? Your scaredness? Tell me more about it," Brunhilde said, spreading her palms flat on the tabletop. "I do not get what you are feeling."

Erik believed her. He also didn't think there was any good way to explain it to her, but trying to was probably the quickest route to boring her and thus having her refocus that intense stare on some new Let's Conquer This project.

"Um . . ." Erik thought about how to describe the feelings he had all the time. He said, "Coaches tell me to look inside myself for courage, but that's not what's in there. My insides are jam-packed with pointy splinters of fear, and there's no room for anything else. When I'm afraid, the fear gets sharper and pointier, and my heart's a running rabbit, and my stomach turns itself inside out. It's not only catching tooth-covered fish that's bad. It feels like . . . everything. There's always something I can't escape. Piano lessons, baseball, talking on the phone, answering questions at school . . . I mean, if I could just AVOID STUFF . . ." He trailed off.

Brunhilde squinted at him as if trying to see through his skin to the fear underneath. She pointed to his bowl. "Do you feel fear splinters right now, eating that oatmeal?" she asked.

He considered it. "Well, no." He lifted his spoon and let the soggy oats drip off it. "I am not afraid of the oatmeal." He looked up at his sister and then quickly looked away. "I am kind of afraid of talking to you about this, but the oats are not a problem."

Brunhilde thought for a moment. "Good. From what you explain, you probably should be afraid of me a little bit." She thought some more. "Everyone should be. But we can take 'eating oatmeal' off the list of things we need to test. Cousins!" she commanded. "To me! I have a plan!"

Hrolf and Ragnar came in a hurry, Ragnar with the two boy triplets under his arms and Hrolf carrying Sally. The cousins knew that whenever Brunhilde came up with a plan, it was bound to involve battles and struggle and other very Viking things.

"A plan? The list of things we need to test?" Erik echoed his sister.

Brunhilde nodded. "This thing you call fear makes very little sense right now. Could it really be caused by 'everything,' as you suggest? Or is there a finite list? We must treat it like any worthy opponent, and prepare for battle with good reconnaissance."

Oh great, Erik thought. *She wants to start one of her Let's Conquer This projects.*

His sister continued, "Fear is your foe, I think. It is your own personal enemy that holds you in its clutches day and night. I cannot help you to attack it until we understand it better. But once I do, routing it out can commence with maximum force. This fear will have nowhere to hide." Her eyes took on a ferocious glow.

Erik's own eyes widened, and he felt a new splintery shard of fear sprout inside him. *Odin's beard,* he thought. *She wants to make ME into one of her Let's Conquer This projects.*

FOUR

THE BIG BOOK OF FEAR

Teeth are both for smiling and for biting. Choose wisely when to do one and not the other.
—The Lore

The rest of the afternoon was taken up with Aunt Hilda coaching Erik and Brunhilde through some of the ins and outs of triplet care. Erik started to yawn uncontrollably after dinner. He tried to hide it, but Aunt Hilda gently observed, "Modern travel really wears a person out. We aren't meant to move such great distances so quickly. Hrolf, show Erik where he'll be sleeping so he can let his soul catch up with his body."

Hrolf escorted Erik to his and Ragnar's room and

reached under the set of bunk beds, rolling out a twin-size trundle bed set neatly tucked with fresh sheets and a knitted blanket.

"There you go," Hrolf said. "Da built it. It's comfortable. I tested it out before you got here."

"Can we push it into a corner?" Erik asked between yawns.

"Sure," said Hrolf said, shoving the bed across the floor until it thumped against the wall. The trundle bed's frame was on wheels about an inch off the floor, so while there was no room for Erik to hide out beneath it, there wasn't any room for any squirrels to hide out beneath it either.

With not even enough energy left to brush his teeth or change clothes, Erik burrowed down into the bedding, pulling the blanket up over his head. His final waking thought was a sincere hope that after a good night's sleep, Brunhilde would forget entirely about her fear-conquering plans.

~

No such luck.

Brunhilde called a meeting of the Sheepflattener

kids the next day. "Brother! Cousins! To me! We need to find information. Some things about fear: how to identify it, where to locate it, and how to exterminate it. The Lore is unlikely to help enough. Other than causing it among our enemies, fear is not a Sheepflattener specialty," she said.

Ragnar nodded, and Hrolf said under his breath, "Oh goody, this is how things started with the geese."

Brunhilde asked Ragnar, "Do you know some wise elders with whom we can consult? Preferably ones from non-Viking lands where they understand these notions of scaredness and fear?"

Erik knew this could get out of hand fast. "Wait, um, I have an idea," he interrupted before Ragnar could lead them to the local US Marines recruitment office. He blurted out the first semi-sane idea that came to him. "You know where they always tell us to go at school when we want to learn something new? The library. You can give me directions to the library, and I'll go there and research this myself. No need for everyone to go."

Libraries were the most under-the-bed-like places he knew. People were forced to be quiet, and he was pretty sure the librarians would not allow any axe-throwing there. His sister and cousins wouldn't choose to spend much time in an axe-forbidding zone if they could help it.

"The library," mused Brunhilde. "A building filled with information. Yes, why not? A fine place to begin. But it is nonsense for you to go forth alone, brother. You have lived too long alone in the shadow of this fear. We rally to your side!" She started to chant a Norse rallying cry but broke off abruptly. "Wait." She sniffed the air. "Before we go." She grabbed Siegmund from his brother and shoved him into Erik's arms. "Here. He needs his diaper changed. Are you fearful now?"

"Uh . . ." Erik wished his sister hadn't decided he needed her help, but at least they were going somewhere that enforced peace and quiet. He looked down at the baby. Now he smelled it too. "Nope, not fearful. Just wondering if all babies smell this much. And why are they so sticky?" he asked, watching Siegmund drool on his hand and then rub it into his hair.

"Mm. It is as you say. Babies are indeed smelly and sticky. But it is helpful to know they are not one of the things that make you scared," Brunhilde said. Erik tried to hand Siegmund back to her, but she crossed her arms. "Since you do not fear it, change the diaper now, before we go."

Erik walked over to the changing table and got to work with the wipes. "Why are you doing this?" he asked his sister.

"Because it is your turn. Aunt Hilda made it clear that we must all help with the triplet diapers. It is too much for any one person to handle."

"No, I mean, why do you want to fix my fears?" His twin sisters never paid Erik much attention. They led busy lives, like every other kid in Ridgewell, Connecticut. He mostly saw them at meals or competitions. And on Saturday nights, when the Sheepflatteners almost always watched a movie together and his mom filled this enormous wooden bowl with fresh-popped, seriously buttered popcorn. That was nice. Otherwise, his sisters sort of treated him like a piece of furniture: always part of the scenery, but not something with which you did much. He wanted to go back to things being that way as soon as possible.

Brunhilde looked into the distance. "I, Brunhilde Sheepflattener, daughter of Inge and Thorfast, granddaughter of Golveg and Vigdis, I am your sister. I will always be on your side and vanquish that which would trouble you. Family takes care of family," she stated.

Erik knew once his sister started reciting her bloodline and using the word *vanquish* that she was going to insist on getting her way. He wasn't going to blend in with any furniture again until they got this over with. He finished cleaning and rebuttoning his small cousin and handed him to Hrolf, who strapped Siegmund into the middle seat of the huge triplet stroller.

"To the library," Brunhilde barked. "Our quest begins!"

~

The library was a modern brick building with lots of windows and colorful posters inviting patrons to READ! Ragnar led the way through the front doors to the children's section. The children and teens department was at the far end of the building and included an inviting play space with dress-up clothes, building toys for little ones, and a larger space with comfy chairs, computers, and a fish tank where older children could relax or do homework.

Mrs. Harkness, the children's librarian, was a round woman with a cap of curly white hair. She beamed at the Sheepflattener clan from behind the ASK ME desk. "What can I help you find today, children?" she asked.

Brunhilde bowed low. "Greetings, wise ruler of the library. We seek an understanding of fear," she said.

"Fear, you say?" Mrs. Harkness typed something into her library catalog computer. "Yes, we have *Fanny Fearless and the Fang* under *F* in picture books. *Fright Club* is over in new YA. And *Oh, a Spear, a Spear I Fear,* of course, that's in poetry."

Hrolf said, "I bet the triplets would like that book about fangs." He pushed the stroller toward the picture books.

Brunhilde shook her head. "No, thank you, we request a book of learning. Nonfiction. Something to explain fear to us so we may wage war against it in the suitable manner."

"Oh my, yes, that's a different kettle of fish," Mrs. Harkness said. She typed some more. "We have *The Big*

Book of Fear, call number 152.46, that should be a start. And if you are waging any sort of war, make sure you pick up Sun Tzu's *The Art of War.* Even though it was written two thousand years ago, it's one of those oldies but goodies. There's a translation for teenagers under TEEN 355.02. Oh, dear, no!" This last comment she directed at Sven and Siegmund, who were trying to gum off pieces of *Fanny Fearless* while Hrolf dangled the book in front of their faces. "That's for reading, not for eating!"

Brunhilde dragged Erik over to the teen nonfiction area. She located the slim book bound in red silk entitled *The Art of War.* She opened it to the first page and read out loud, *"War is . . . the road to survival or ruin. It is mandatory that it be thoroughly studied."* She grunted in approval. "Oh, I like this one."

While his sister was distracted by flipping through war advice, Erik crept away and hid in the dress-up corner. His hiding spot didn't last long. When Brunhilde emerged from her absorption in the ancient Chinese text, she tugged him out from under a pile of superhero capes and princess dresses and hauled him over to the first row of nonfiction books. She wasn't getting bored with the library anywhere near as quickly as he had thought she would.

Erik said, "How is a book going to help with anything? It doesn't seem very Viking to use a book to learn to attack stuff." Maybe he could sidetrack his sister with an argument about Vikingness.

Brunhilde didn't take the bait. "Seeking knowledge is very Viking. Learning from great teachers can lead any of us to be a better warrior, whether a teaching is carved on a stone or written in an encyclopedia or filmed on YouTube." She paused. "Do not tell Mom I said that. She is so partial to stone carvings."

Brunhilde examined book spines until she came upon the 152.46 section and pulled a thick caramel-colored volume off the shelf. *The Big Book of Fear* was embossed in black letters on the cover. Brunhilde sat down in the aisle and inspected its table of contents. "It is an alphabetical list of fears," she said. "So many of them. Who would have thought?" She turned to the introduction and scanned it. "The writer says here their scientific term is *phobias,* from the original Greek word for being scared." She flipped through to the *A* section.

"Okay. We begin. Do you have Ablutophobia? Acaropho-bia? Algophobia? Agoraphobia? Aibohphobia?"

Erik looked around to see if anyone was staring at them. They were alone in the nonfiction section. He sat down next to her. "I don't have any idea what those things mean."

His sister riffled through a few more pages. "Nor do I. Explaining and testing these would take years of summer vacations. It seems we need a more concentrated plan. We must know your adversary better without delay." She hunted through her satchel and pulled out a purple notebook and glittery pen. She flipped past pages with sketches of weapons and battle strategies to a fresh page, which she labeled *ERIK VS. FEAR*. "Let us first list the possible fears of which you are aware. What do you wish never to face again?"

"Piano lessons," Erik blurted. "Baseball and hockey and soccer . . . I guess any team sport at all. Going to school. Walking in the woods where squirrels can run loose."

She wrote quickly. "And?"

"Riding the bus. Fishing with my bare hands.

Bleeding. Talking on the phone. Answering the phone. Hearing a phone ring anywhere for any reason."

She held her palm up. "That is enough to start." She flipped to the index in the back of the book and searched. "Here we are," she said, and continued taking notes. "Melophobia, fear of music. Athlemaphobia, fear of sports. Didaskaleinophobia, fear of school. Sciurophobia, fear of squirrels. Nothing about buses, but there's hodophobia, fear of travel. Ichthyophobia, fear of fish. Hemophobia, fear of blood. Fear of phones is . . . telephonophobia." She smiled. "Ha. That one is funny."

"Seriously?" Erik was impressed in spite of himself. "All of those are actually written down in there?"

Brunhilde was now numbering Erik's list of possible fears. "I told you. It is best to perform reconnaissance first to establish the parameters of your enemy: their names, history, heritage, locations, strengths, and weaknesses. We can now run field tests."

"Field tests?"

"Yes. Testing these in real life. For example, we can take you to the local school and witness which aspects of school bother you. We can go to the pet store and observe which fish you find most upsetting. Perhaps the store will also have squirrels to which we can expose you."

Erik whimpered.

Brunhilde continued, "As the leader of this expedition, I say we will begin with . . . hmmm . . . piano lessons. Since piano lessons were the first fear that leapt to your mind, there may be some significance to that. We will test each aspect of a piano lesson to determine exactly where your fear originates. We will do this for all of your phobias.

"Then —" She slammed the book closed. "We attack."

~

After checking out their books and heading home from the library, they were occupied for the rest of the evening with triplet care and dinner preparations. It took an astonishing amount of time to help Aunt Hilda and Uncle Bjorn feed, bathe, and cuddle the three babies to sleep. The triplets were like falling dominoes. If one started eating, they all had to eat. If one started crying, they all had to cry. If one needed his diaper changed, it was a circus of diapers and wipes and the cousins doing

Rock Paper Daggers to determine whose turn it was to handle which triplet.

Once the babies were settled, Aunt Hilda got the older cousins working together to prepare a meal of sardine and mushroom stew. After dinner and cleanup, everyone turned in for the night. Hrolf and Ragnar were snoring as soon as their heads hit their pillows. Erik expected he'd stay awake worrying about what the next day would bring. What did his sister mean when she said she needed to test each aspect of his fears? Why did she have to focus her everything-is-a-battle brain on him? But instead of getting swirled up into a worryfest, baby care had worn him out. He fell asleep almost as quickly as his cousins had.

When he awoke, dawn was barely brightening the sky. Hrolf's and Ragnar's beds were empty, and he could hear his aunt and uncle talking in the kitchen. He wished he could stay under the covers all day with the two Garfield books he'd gotten at the library, but he knew hiding in bed while his cousins and sister took care of the triplets was not an option.

He crept out of bed and into the kitchen, and found

Brunhilde stirring a pot of oatmeal. She greeted Erik with the words "Prepare yourself. Testing begins today."

Erik looked to the grownups, hoping they might give the kids complicated housework jobs that would take up the whole day. Instead, Aunt Hilda told them to enjoy each other's company while she foraged for wild greens and Uncle Bjorn chopped down trees to prepare an addition to the house. Once the breakfast dishes were washed and dried, they left the older children in charge of the triplets until lunchtime.

Brunhilde commanded the other Sheepflatteners to gather on the rug near the living room's stereo and piano. Like a general positioning her troops, she strategically arranged Hrolf, Ragnar, and the triplets, and instructed Erik to sit on the piano bench.

"You have a stereo and a piano?" Erik asked Ragnar. The stereo and piano were pretty old-fashioned, but they stood out as super modern against the house's other furnishings.

"Sure. Ma says we're Vikings, not barbarians," Ragnar said.

"Quiet, everyone! Focus yourselves. Test number one,"

Brunhilde announced as she wrote the header *ERIK VS. PIANO LESSONS* on a fresh notebook page. "Melophobia, fear or hatred of music." She stood directly beside the bench and glowered down at Erik. "Play something."

Erik plunked out most of the notes of a scale and looked up.

"More," she insisted.

He played a major chord, then a minor chord. He tapped out as much as he could remember of "The Funny Little Bunny," followed by a few mistake-riddled renditions of "The Happy Halibut."

Brunhilde raised her eyebrows, and Erik shrugged.

"Hmmm. Interesting," she said, writing something down with her glittery pen. "All right. Part two of testing melophobia," she continued. "Let us next listen to 'The Ride of the Valkyries,' a piece of music written about our foremothers. Now, *this* is the sound of an assaulting force." She cued Ragnar to press Play on the stereo.

Exciting music began flowing from the speakers. Nervous flutes and other high woodwinds were chirping and tweeting while forceful violins and violas sliced through them like swords through songbirds. Deeper strings like cellos and double basses started galloping along, and a French horn section joined in.

Brunhilde rubbed her arms and closed her eyes. "I love this part," she said. She opened her eyes and checked on Erik. "Are you fearful now?"

Erik shook his head. A whole host of trumpets and trombones joined the French horns.

"Louder," Brunhilde ordered Ragnar. He turned the volume knob. The horns began soaring upward and demanding to be heard and admired. The cousins listened for several more minutes to the harmonies blasting out of the stereo.

"Now?" Brunhilde asked again.

Erik checked each of his body parts. No sense of fear splinters stabbing him from within. "Nothing yet," he said.

Brunhilde walked over to stereo herself and turned up the volume knob to eleven. The rising theme was now played by different instruments trading off. The music swirled up, fell down, and crashed in triumph. Brunhilde's arms were covered with goose bumps, and she was showing her teeth with what could have been happiness or something much less pleasant. After more swirling and crashing waves of sound, a woman began to sing on the recording, and Brunhilde paused the CD.

"WELL?" she asked her brother in the ringing silence.

"I THINK I MIGHT BE A LITTLE DEAF NOW," Erik answered. "BUT I AM NOT AFRAID."

Brunhilde took out her notebook and checked off *No* next to *melophobia*. "The whole *Ring des Nibelungen* opera cycle is more than fourteen hours long, but we just listened to the best part. If that doesn't bother you, I don't think any music will. So it is not music that makes you afraid of your music lessons. And you sat right next to that piano the whole time as well, meaning it is not the mere presence of a piano. What else establishes the circumstances of a piano lesson?"

Erik considered this while the ringing in his ears diminished. What made a piano lesson a *piano lesson*?

"I'm alone in a room with a piano, a music book, a metronome, and Mrs. Loathcraft. She tells me to play, and I try, and then she tells me how bad I am at it."

"I see. Could it be sitting in a room with an old

woman?" She flipped through *The Big Book of Fear.* "That is called gerontophobia, fear of old people."

Erik pictured Harriet P. Loathcraft in his head, peering over his shoulder as he fumbled through "The Happy Halibut" for the millionth time. His throat seized up. "Yeah," he wheezed. "That might be it."

"Right." Brunhilde grabbed his arm and dragged him to his feet.

Erik said, "Wait, what? Mrs. Loathcraft is hundreds of miles away."

Undeterred, Brunhilde kept ahold of his arm and tossed her braids over her shoulder with a flick of her head. "We have many elderly people at our disposal here in Minnesota, I am sure. Ragnar? Where is your nearest depository of old piano teachers?"

Ragnar looked at Hrolf. They whispered together for a moment. "The library was full of old people reading newspapers," Ragnar offered.

"Excellent," said Brunhilde. "We can also get another Fanny Fearless book for the triplets. They are quite amusing."

FIVE

FIND YOUR PHOBIA

That which is hidden in the snow
turns up in the thaw.
— The Lore

B ack at the town library, Hrolf wheeled the triplets to the picture book nook. Erik and Brunhilde hung out near the entrance while Ragnar scouted ahead in the periodicals room to find an old person with whom to confront Erik. He came back shaking his head. "One mother with a baby and a sleeping teenager, that's it."

Brunhilde tapped her cheek. "What about the head of the children's department?" She turned to Erik. "Is she enough like Mrs. Loathcraft for you?"

"Oh yeah," interjected Ragnar. "Mrs. Harkness. She's a musician too. She performs some kind of music around town, I forget what exactly. Maybe it's piano. Or is it bagpipes? They sound a lot alike."

Erik mumbled, "C'mon, I don't really think we should bother the children's librarian—" But Ragnar yanked him along past the circulation desk and behind a display of new mystery paperbacks. Ragnar peered around the books over toward the children's ASK ME desk. Mrs. Harkness was inside her glass-fronted office, examining the torn cover on a board book and measuring out some tape to repair it.

"White curly hair . . . wrinkles . . . purple-rimmed glasses on a chain," Ragnar whispered to Erik. "She's humming something too. That's musical, right? Is she a good one? Will she scare you?"

"Hey, just because she looks something like Mrs. Loathcraft doesn't mean that we need to involve her—"

"Erik says she looks like his piano teacher. Let's do this thing," Ragnar said to Brunhilde.

"One, two, three, and up we go," Brunhilde said, and she and Ragnar each gripped one of Erik's elbows and carried him past the read-aloud section and the reshelving cart right through Mrs. Harkness's office door. Erik didn't even have a moment to stutter out a protest.

"Well, hello, children, what can I help you find today?" Mrs. Harkness beamed up at them from her office chair. "I trust you are enjoying *The Big Book of Fear*?" The damaged book in her hands was entitled *Goodnight Goon* with creepy little monsters peeking through a window.

Brunhilde said, "He is all yours." She and Ragnar dropped Erik's arms and backed out of the office. Brunhilde pulled the door shut behind them with an ominous *click*.

Erik forced a laugh. "Ha, ha, they are . . . um, playing a little joke. I'm sorry, I'll be going now." He tried the doorknob and found it locked. He tried pulling it open, but the heavy door wouldn't budge. Through the large window, he saw Brunhilde and Ragnar standing back behind the mystery paperback display, observing him with serious faces. Brunhilde had her purple notebook out, and her glittery pen was poised above the page. Ragnar had *The Big Book of Fear* under one arm.

"How do I unlock this door?" Erik asked.

"That's odd." Mrs. Harkness frowned. "I don't have a lock on my office door." She came around her desk and tried the knob herself, shaking it back and forth as it rattled in the door frame. She peered down at the mechanism. "There appears to be something metal jammed in there . . . a sardine can key? How peculiar." She returned to her chair and opened up a drawer packed with odds and ends. "I probably have a tool in here somewhere we can use to get that loose." She pulled out a flashlight, an individually wrapped Twizzler, a mechanical pencil, and pack of sticky notes with the word *Shhhhh!* written across the top. "Come on over, sonny, and help me look."

Erik was still looking out the window at Brunhilde and Ragnar, shaking his head in disbelief and spreading his hands in the universal symbol of *What are you doing?* Brunhilde narrowed her eyes and jabbed her glittery pen toward him in a spinning motion, as if to say, *Get going and get yourself scared.*

He turned back around to see if Mrs. Harkness had

located a tool for unjamming the door from the frame. She waved him over to the other side of the desk, where another full drawer awaited inspection. "There's a screwdriver around here somewhere, I'm pretty sure," she said. "Look under the lollipops."

Erik started pawing through the lollipop drawer, unearthing a giant wrench, a mallet, and a set of tiny plastic frogs, but no screwdriver. "Not here."

"No? Oh, I know, let's call maintenance and have them come take care of it," she said. She picked up the phone and listened to it for a moment. She pressed a bunch of buttons and jiggled the hook switch. "Well, I'll be, the line's dead. This just isn't our lucky day."

Erik glared out of the window and saw Ragnar waving the cut end of a wire at him and smiling. His rune tattoo today said CRUSH. Erik raised his hands again and gestured to say, *Why do I need to be locked in with a phoneless librarian? What do you expect me to do?* Brunhilde scribbled something, ignoring his silent pleas.

Mrs. Harkness was undaunted. "Well, the maintenance room is around the corner. We need to get their attention. You look like you have nice young, healthy lungs. Let's yell until they hear us. I don't normally say this in the library, but feel free to use your outside voice." She exclaimed, "Yoo-hoo! Mr. Ingersold! Harry! A little help in the children's room! Yoo-hoo, yoo-hoo, yoo-hoo!"

No one appeared. She cleared her throat and said, "Guess we'll need to be a little louder than that. Well, I'm up for the challenge. I'm the county's top senior-category yodeler, I'll have you know."

Mrs. Harkness started yodeling. And this was not any I'm-being-cute-during-storytime-for-little-kids-type yodeling. This was full-throated, high-pitched, all-over-the-scale hooting and hollering. Her voice echoed off the glass and multiplied. The little kids in the dress-up area toddled over to stare. Still in the triplet stroller, Sven hid under *Fanny Fearless Faces a Ferret*. Mrs. Harkness paused in her ululations, patted Erik between his shoulder blades, and said, "Come on, make some noise. I promise you won't get in any trouble with *this* librarian!" She inhaled and kept on warbling.

They now had quite a crowd gathered. Adults from the mystery paperback shelf had wandered over to stare along with the kids. All those eyes peering through the big glass window. Erik's heart began to pound, and he felt like a powerful gust of wind was blowing through his insides. The urge to sink down and slide under Mrs. Harkness's desk was nearly overpowering. His knees began to buckle. He put one hand on a stack of new hardbacks to steady himself as a maintenance worker strode over with a tool belt and a smile, waving and calling out, "I'm here, I'm here, Lillian. Tell me what you need."

Mrs. Harkness waved back through the glass. "There you are, Harry! Knew that'd get you to come running. That was the yodeling piece that won me top senior status at last year's competition. Anyhoo, we've got a stuck door and an out-of-order phone. Can you get us out of here?" she asked.

As soon as the yodeling librarian quieted back down into a regular librarian, the crowd lost interest and ambled away. Erik's heart eased slightly from a gallop to a trot, and he wiped the sweat off his forehead. Brunhilde was at his side the moment the sardine key popped free and the door opened, shepherding him over to a comfy chair.

"It worked, did it not?" she said. "We have isolated

something that scares you. Now the debriefing." She sat on the arm of the chair and consulted her notebook. "You functioned normally when you found the locked door and the cut phone line, displaying only signs of irritation. Being trapped with a senior-category lady was not overwhelming your defenses. But when she began to — er — sing? You turned white as quartz."

As much as Erik wanted to grumble at Brunhilde for putting him such a bizarre situation, grumbling at Brunhilde had never gotten anyone anywhere. He said, "I was okay until she started up with the yoda-lay-hee-hoos. Then I started to get sweaty. She wanted me to yodel along with her."

"Yodeling-with-an-old-person-aphobia?" Ragnar asked. "Is that in the book?" He started to fumble through the index with his bear-size hands.

But Erik shook his head. "It wasn't the yodeling. It was . . . everyone looking at her while she was yodeling. And everyone looking at me right next to her." All those curious eyeballs trained on him. "I couldn't stand everyone staring at me with nowhere to hide. I didn't want to be there. I didn't want to be . . . embarrassed."

He considered it some more. "Yeah, *embarrassed* is the word, for sure. Being embarrassed in front of other people is awful. Really awful." He hoped this would satisfy his sister.

Brunhilde took the book from Ragnar, scanned the index, and pointed to the *K* section of *The Big Book of Fear.* "Katagelophobia. Fear of embarrassment, ridicule, or being put down. From the Greek language, *kata* means to put down and *gelo* means laughing. Are you certain this has nothing to do with old people?"

Hrolf had rejoined them with the triplets. Ragnar poked Hrolf in the chest with a hairy finger and said, "Laugh at your cousin."

Hrolf shrugged, pointed at Erik, and started laughing. Siegmund and Sally seemed to think this was a lovely idea and joined in, until a ribbon of mucus spilled out of Sally's nose and she tried to use Siegmund as a tissue and Ragnar had to start laughing as well. (Sven stayed quiet. He still held the Fanny Fearless book open over his head like a small tent, his watchful eyes tracking Mrs. Harkness.) Once again, a crowd started turning and staring their way. Erik lost no time in sliding as far as he could under the comfy chair and whispering, "Please stop. PLEASE. Fear of embarrassment is most definitely IT."

Brunhilde's eyes shone. "Our journey toward victory begins. We have named your enemy. With naming comes power. Your fear is no longer just fear. It is" — she paused triumphantly — "katagelophobia."

SIX

WHAT LIES UNDERNEATH

*Even the one-finned fish can
fight against the current.*
— The Lore

B ut it isn't just katagelophobia," Ragnar said.

"Mmmm," answered Brunhilde around a mouthful of catfish hot dish. Brunhilde and Ragnar had heated up some lunch for everyone while Aunt Hilda helped Uncle Bjorn prune branches outside in a light drizzle. The triplets sat in three matching ExerSaucers on the floor, slurping their bottles. "Interesting. What do you mean?"

Ragnar answered, "You said Erik was scared of the

pike at the lake. Being bitten by a pike isn't embarrassing, I don't think. It's more like . . ."

"Aaaack!" screamed Erik, jumping up onto the seat of his chair, eyes nearly bulging out of his head. "How did *that* get in here?" He pointed at an animal on the floor.

"What, Mr. Nubbins?" asked Hrolf. "He's our pet. He must've gotten out of his cage."

Mr. Nubbins wasn't a big squirrel, nor a very hearty-looking one. He was missing part of one ear, and the fur on his tail was falling out. His eyes darted, and he made a nervous gnawing sound with his teeth. He sprinted toward an open window, but before he made it across the room, Sven dropped his bottle, reached out, and grabbed him by the neck, pulling him onto the ExerSaucer's Busy Boy Control Center. Mr. Nubbins drooped in defeat. Sven gurgled happily, stuck the squirrel's good ear between his gums, and chomped.

"You have a squirrel living in your house? It's a wild animal!" yelled Erik, gripping his chair back with white knuckles. "That's insane! Get it out of here, get it out, get it OUT!" He was trembling so hard from head to foot that his chair chattered against the floor.

"See?" said Ragnar. "I don't think he's fearful of being embarrassed by Mr. Nubbins."

"Indeed," answered Brunhilde. "Good thinking, Ragnar." She strode over to Sven and took Mr. Nubbins from his moist little hands. Sven frowned until he found his brother Siegmund's hand and shoved that into his mouth to continue chewing.

Brunhilde approached Erik with the squirrel as the critter flicked drool off its Sven-sucked ear. "So, Erik, what exactly bothers you about this animal? Are you thinking it will harm you?" She examined Mr. Nubbins's face and paws.

"Get it AWAY from me, Bru, RIGHT NOW!" Of the fears he had mentioned to Brunhilde, this was the one he most did not want to test. *Squirrels,* he thought. *Is there anything on earth more awful than fast-moving, nut-crunching, tail-twitching squirrels?*

Brunhilde said, "I can assure you that its teeth and claws are very, very small. Even you, with little practice in hand-to-hand combat, could defend yourself against it if necessary. The amount of your blood it could spill would be quite minor." She moved closer to show Erik

Mr. Nubbins's little furry nose and black eyes. The creature's tail twitched.

Erik climbed right through his plate of catfish to stand in the middle of the table. He forgot that he never yelled at Brunhilde and yelled at Brunhilde, "I'm going to start screaming again if you don't get it AWAY! I AM SERIOUS! I DON'T CARE! GET THAT THING AWAY FROM ME!!" He clutched his hair with both hands and panted like a dog.

Brunhilde stopped and gazed at her brother yelling and panting at her from atop the dining room table. She nodded once and took the squirrel out of the room. When she returned, her hands were empty.

"He is back in his cage. No need to concern yourself any longer about Mr. Nubbins, Erik. You may relax from combat mode." She brushed squirrel fur from her hands and sat back down to lunch.

Erik was having a hard time calming down. His breathing was still shallow and rapid, his skin felt cold and clammy. Ragnar stood up and wrapped his big hands around Erik's waist, lifting him down to his chair and patting him on the head.

"I guess we need to add squirrelophobia to his list, huh?" Ragnar said.

"Sciurophobia," Brunhilde corrected him absently. "It's named sciurophobia. We found it in the book already." She quickly finished the last bites from her plate and moved it to the side. "I wonder how many fears a person can have?" She grabbed her notebook from her nearby bookbag and began to sketch out a battlefield with *X*'s and *O*'s and arrows. "Perhaps your fears are separate, or perhaps they work together to undermine you."

The phone rang. Erik, already on the verge of running out of the squirrel-infested house, yelled, "Gaaah!" and sprinted for the front door. He pulled it open to a thunderclap and cascade of rain. He slammed it shut and scuttled under the couch, tucking himself in a tight ball as far underneath it as he could.

Hrolf said, "Da said Erik didn't know about the pleasure of having to fight, but it looks like he's fighting this fear thing almost all the time."

Brunhilde agreed. "Cousin, you speak the truth. I am glad we are here together to help him face this. Although it is a well-entrenched enemy, nothing can stand against the Sheepflatteners united as one." Even the triplets joined in the proud family grunting.

Aunt Hilda walked in with her phone. "Brunhilde and Erik, good news! Your mother called, and your sister Allyson is coming to Minnesota on Saturday to join us. Her cheer team qualified for a big competition out here. I'll have to plan a menu and rearrange the beds and make some room in the closets." Aunt Hilda sighed happily in anticipation of another guest. Her rune tattoo was the same as Inge's: FAMILY. "Wait, where is Erik?"

"Hiding under the couch," Brunhilde said. "Telephone calls sometimes make him do that. It might be katagelophobia, or it might be something else. I don't think it relates to sciurophobia, but one way or another, we are going to root out the truth."

"Oh. Ah. Hmm," said Aunt Hilda. "Well, carry on." She scooped up Sven in one arm and Siegmund in the other and used her foot to scoot Sally's ExerSaucer toward the bedrooms. "It's nappy-nap time for you, my tiny warriors!"

Hrolf crawled over on his hands and knees to the

couch and peeked at Erik. "Want to come out now? Or I can come under there with you, and we can play Sharkie, Sharkie, Cross My Couch."

Erik had no idea what Sharkie, Sharkie, Cross My Couch was, but if it was something his Minnesota cousins played, he was not up for it. He whispered, "How do I know that squirrel won't get out of his cage? Can you put the cage in a closet? And lock the door? And bury the key?"

"I can take care of locking up Mr. Nubbins for you," said Hrolf, grinning. "The triplets and I can play No Escape from Jotunheim, Land of Giants, with him after their nap. I'll be the biggest giant, they can be my giants-in-training, and we can pretend Mr. Nubbins is our sworn mini-giant enemy who must not be allowed to break free. We'll use Legos."

Hrolf offered him a hand, and Erik reluctantly took it. Hrolf had almost pulled him out from under the couch when the phone rang once more. Erik yelled, "Gaaah!" broke Hrolf's grip, and recoiled backwards like an eel. Hrolf peeked under the couch again and saw only a faint balled-up-Erik-shaped shadow. He shrugged and headed off to begin constructing the Land of Giants for after naptime.

Another set of boots appeared at the edge of Erik's vision.

"Erik," Brunhilde said. "Time for another test."

"Bru, no," he moaned. "I'm too scared for testing."

"Ah, scared is perfect. We are going to get at what scares you about the phone ringing."

Ragnar came in holding the phone. "It's Allyson. She's calling to ask Brunhilde what kind of clothes she should pack for her visit."

"Excellent." Brunhilde took the cell phone from him and spoke into it. "Allyson, I am going to have you talk to Erik." She crouched down and offered the phone to him under the couch. He tried to push it away, but she gave him a hard look. He took the call.

"Hi, Allyson," he said softly.

"Erik? Hi? So, like, I was going to pack my cashmere tees and skinny jeans and black leather boots, but then I was wondering if the other girls out there are more into pastel sweats and mountain-climber capris and hats? Is everyone out there wearing lots of hats? Should I bring all my hats? Or just the ones with matching infinity scarves?"

"Um."

"Or, like, should I pack just everything, just, like, everything? Because different situations may call for different looks? And will Aunt Hilda let me wear makeup? Or is she in the dark ages like Mom and I have to wait until I'm sixteen?"

"Well . . ."

"Okay, I'll bring it all. Don't want to be caught without the best look for the situation, right? Thanks, little bro! You're totes helpful! Buh-bye!"

"Buh-bye," Erik answered. He poked his head out and looked up at Bru, who had her notebook in her hand and was sketching something.

"Wait!" Brunhilde said, and grabbed the phone. "Allyson? Are you still there? Good. Please, can you call us back in ten minutes? Okay? Thank you." She pressed the End Call button.

Erik crawled out from under the couch and sat on the floor. "You're going to make me talk to her again in ten minutes? I don't think I'm going to have a better clue what to say to her about clothes in ten minutes."

"No, you will not need to talk to her. But the ten minutes gives us a chance to examine your phone-ringing fear in a way you normally cannot." She had written down a series of questions and began peppering Erik with them.

"Was talking to Allyson scary?"

"No."

"Was it embarrassing?"

"No. Confusing, mostly, I guess."

"Do you ever *not* yell 'gaaah!' when the phone rings?"

"No."

"I know you have been yelping at phone calls as long as I have known you. When the phone rings at our house, I wait for your 'gaaah!' right afterward so I know for sure it really rang. Are you always scared to hear it ring?"

"Well, yeah."

"Is the phone ringing embarrassing?"

He frowned. "No, that's not it."

"Does the phone ringing remind you of squirrels?"

"No!" Erik said. "That's just silly."

"So, what does a ringing phone make you feel?"

Erik thought about it. "Instant terror. Like I was just minding my own business and then suddenly, an alarm is going off to tell me I'm in danger. Or like I was hiding from a monster in the dark but then it shines a flashlight right on me and I'm caught."

Brunhilde was writing every word of this down. ". . . And you are caught. Like a predator or enemy has located you and there is no escape?"

"Yep."

She handed him the as-yet-not-ringing phone. He took it.

"Does it appear monstrous or predatory to you now when it is silent?"

He examined it. "Nope."

Ragnar joined in, grabbing the triplets' toy telephone, which had a smiling face painted on it and, when dragged along the floor, would play "Pop Goes the Weasel."

"How about this one?" He pressed a button, and little blue and red lights on the phone lit up. He held it up to his ear. "Hello? Hello?"

Erik stared at him. "No, I think it has to be a real phone ringing for a real phone call."

"Okay." Brunhilde nodded. "We are getting closer. Why does a real phone ring? Because a person is calling to tell us something, or ask us something. Think about that, Erik. Allyson is going to call in one minute to ask us more about clothes. Does that make you feel the monster-predator terror?"

Erik looked at the phone and imagined it ringing in his hand with Allyson's voice on the other end babbling on about hats and scarves. The zing of fear he normally got didn't appear.

"No, thinking about that doesn't bother me."

"Okay. Brace yourself. It should be ringing again any second."

Right on cue, the phone rang in his hand, and he twitched, but didn't yelp. It rang again. He didn't yelp again. Erik's mouth dropped open in silent disbelief at its own silence. "I can't believe it! No 'gaaah!' First time ever!" The phone rang one more time. "Should I answer it?"

"No," Brunhilde ordered. "Now imagine this—what

if it is not Allyson on the phone right now? What if it is someone else calling for some other reason? How would you feel about it then?"

Erik dropped the phone. "Oh no," he wheezed. "That puts me right back in the monster-terror place."

Ragnar launched into action. He folded his right hand into a boulder-like fist and punched the phone once, decisively. It stopped ringing altogether. In fact, it looked like it would never ring again. He leaned over and patted Erik on the shoulder. "Maybe you should punch it when it bugs you. That is what I would do if I had a predator showing up and ringing at me. Grab it! And punch it!"

Brunhilde thumped Ragnar on the arm with the toy phone, and it played *All around the mulberry bush, the monkey chased the weasel.* "I was about to get to the bottom of this, cousin. It was not time to punch anything yet," she said.

Ragnar said, "Maybe it wasn't time to punch the phone, but I am pretty sure it is always time to punch something."

Erik said, "Actually, that did help, Ragnar. At least

it stopped ringing. I can't think clearly once it rings at me." He turned to Brunhilde. "So, did we figure out that I'm scared of ringing phones when the call is from an unknown person calling for an unknown reason?" Maybe they were done with this particular testing and he could go back to hiding under the couch again.

Brunhilde said, "You tell me. Is that right? What if it is an unknown person calling to tell you that you have, I don't know, won an award? Or a friend wants to invite you to a party? It could even have nothing to do with you. It could be a call for Allyson. At our house, it usually *is* a call for Allyson."

Erik shook his head. "Even though I know it might not be for me . . . I also know it might. And a ringing phone could never bring me any good news," he said. "If someone was calling to invite me to a party, that would be horrible. Parties are where I fall down roller-skating or miss the piñata. But it's more likely going to be a teacher or coach calling to criticize something I did. Or it will be Mom explaining she just signed me up to go fail at some new activity."

"So you feel sure every phone call brings bad news of past failures or new chances to fail?" Brunhilde worked on the sketch in her notebook. She drew a phone with a spear and labeled it *FAILURE*. "Or maybe you feel every phone call is an opportunity to be criticized?" She drew another phone with an enormous two-handed sword labeled *CRITICISM*.

Ragnar added, "But it *could* be news that your town has been invaded by predatory monsters, and able-bodied men and women must take up arms and defend themselves to the bloody end!"

"That would be cool," Hrolf said. He had returned from setting up the Land of Giants.

Brunhilde said, "It would indeed."

Ragnar swept the pieces of the phone under an armchair. He was losing interest in the discussion. "Want to practice some axe-throwing in the rain?" he asked. "Good training for foul-weather fighting. It looks nice and muddy out there already."

"Just let me get my helmet," Brunhilde said.

"Me too!" added Hrolf.

Erik shook his head and rubbed his eyes. "Not me. I'm going to lie down on this couch now. I'm wiped out from the ringing and squirrels and stuff."

"Fine." Brunhilde shrugged into a rain slicker and pulled on some long leather gloves. "We will finish this later and see if there is a phobia regarding failure or criticism in *The Big Book*. One last question. Do you think we should test your fear of furry long-tailed rodents in more detail? Do you think there is any different, more interesting fear underlying that?"

"What? Wait. Whoa," Erik said. "That one I don't have to think about. We figured out that fear on the first try." *What underlies my fear of squirrels?* he thought as he lay down on the couch, putting a pillow over his face. *More squirrels. It's squirrels all the way down. Squirrels alllll the way down.*

SEVEN

THINGS TO CRITICIZE

If you must bite the hand that feeds
you, wait until after lunchtime.
— The Lore

Brunhilde showed Erik a chapter entitled "People Phobias" in *The Big Book of Fear* the next morning after they finished washing and drying the oatmeal bowls.

"There is a fear of failure named atychiphobia. But see here, there is a whole group of related fears about talking to other people. I am pondering whether you have allodoxaphobia, which is a fear of other people's opinions of you, or enissophobia, a fear of being criticized.

Or both. I thought we could take some time this morning to go to the park and suggest that strangers offer their opinions on you, and then ask other strangers to find something to criticize about you. I will take notes on which one you find more excruciating."

Hrolf offered, "If it helps, I can make a Things to Criticize list they can choose from. They could criticize your hair, or your weird shoes, or the way you talk, or how you dry dishes —"

Erik groaned. "Look, I really don't want to go to the park to have strangers make me feel terrible." He felt just as hopeless as he did saying, "Mom, noooo," before some new activity. Maybe even more hopeless. He'd thought his mother was the worst at ignoring his "no" until he'd become Brunhilde's summer project.

"Go to the park? No park today, children." Uncle Bjorn strode into the room. Erik exhaled gratefully. "I need all hands on deck to sink the lodge poles today, and tomorrow I expect to get a good start on the walls. Hilda has an idea that if we can get the new room framed up before Allyson gets here, she can help add something called 'designer flair,' whatever that may be. So everyone get your boots on. It's a fine day to get out there and sweat as a family."

And sweat they did. The family was kept busy from sunup to dusk for the next several days. They didn't even go inside for meals. Instead, they used pine needles and dry branches to start small fires outside, over which they boiled fresh eggs in their shells and grilled wild turkey sausages. The triplets spent the days with them in a chicken-coop-like playpen, occasionally escaping and wiggling inch by slow inch toward the woods, but someone always picked them up before they made it too far.

Erik had never thought he'd be thankful to spend hours chopping, shaping, and lugging wood, but the aches and pains of hard physical work weren't too bad. Blistered palms seemed to him to be a better fate than blistered feelings.

He watched Brunhilde splitting logs, her braids flying. He didn't like to admit it, but the way she had gotten to the bottom of his fear of embarrassment and fear of phone calls was kind of cool. Knowing he had specific fears rather than a generalized fear of everything might actually be useful. He could focus more on what stuff he needed to avoid when he was planning to AVOID STUFF —instead of feeling like everything on earth was out to get him.

Even so, he still wished his sister would decide she'd done enough, but there was no way to predict when that would happen. Once Brunhilde made up her mind about something, she was like a massive train chugging toward her chosen station, nearly impossible to derail. If only there was some Lore encouraging her to sit around and read comic books, or to make popcorn and watch a movie with her siblings. What was the medieval equivalent of reading books and watching movies? Maybe listening to storytellers?

He said out loud, *"Make plenty of time to hear stories and eat corn exploded over the fire. Skimp not on the butter and salt, and happiness shall be yours,"* earning a weird look from Aunt Hilda. Making up convincing Erik-style Lore was not easy.

Erik carried a stack of kindling over to Uncle Bjorn, who sent him around to the front of the house to rake up some wood chips. Erik got to work, stopping every few minutes to scan the yard for neighborhood squirrels. Luckily, all he spotted was a handful of chickadees and a chipmunk. He was brooding over what made squirrels scarier than other backyard wildlife — he thought it was something about the tail — when a school bus came trundling up the dirt road that led past his uncle's house.

The bus came to stop not far from Erik, and the door clunked open. The driver, a woman with spiky hair and thick mascara, leaned forward and called out, "Hey there, kid, think you could give us directions to Lake Park? We seem to have taken a wrong turn somewhere." Erik was already backing away and shaking his head, ready to run and get someone else to help her, when he felt himself propelled forward by a firm arm around his shoulders. The firm arm had a sweat-smeared rune tattoo of the word CONQUER.

"How fortunate," murmured Brunhilde in his ear. "A chance to test your school bus fear, delivered to our door." How had she gotten around the house so quickly? His sister was sneakier than a squirrel herself.

"Brunhilde, no," he said.

"Yes," she answered.

"No. No, no, no," he replied. "No."

"Oh yes. Really quite yes," his sister insisted.

A moment later, the two of them were up the bus steps and standing at the head of the aisle, looking at a troop of wide-eyed Girl Scouts. *Why doesn't my family listen when I say no?* Erik thought. *Do they not know the meaning of the word* no*?* Then Brunhilde began shoving him down the aisle, and his heart-hammering fear of school buses took over and he stopped knowing exactly what was going on. He heard a lot of confused Scouts asking, "What's wrong with him? Does he need first aid?" He thought at some point he may have made a break for the emergency exit at the back, but tripped and ended up collapsing face first onto a green vinyl seat next to two freaked-out girls. Then he faintly heard the driver announce that they'd find their own way, just please get off of her bus.

Brunhilde hoisted a limp Erik over her shoulder and fireman-carried him back down the steps. She lowered him to the ground and bowed to the driver and Scouts. "Thank you for your service to my brother," she said.

Silent, staring Girl Scouts lined every window as the big yellow vehicle drove away. None of them waved goodbye.

"That was quite successful. I assume you will agree we can categorize bus riding under the fear of embarrassment AND criticism," Brunhilde said.

"I don't know what just happened, I don't want to know what just happened, and I don't want to categorize anything," said Erik, wobbling on uncertain legs.

They walked around back and rejoined the rest of the family. Erik sat on the ground, not ready to get back to work just yet.

Brunhilde said to Ragnar, "We were testing Erik's school bus phobia, and it reminded me to ask: where can we go to test his fear of school itself?"

Ragnar paused in his hammering and leaned one shoulder against the partially finished wall. Erik noticed he'd changed his rune tattoo from CRUSH back to SMASH. Ragnar said, "We're homeschooled, you know. Not sure exactly where the school is. I think it's closed for the summer anyway."

"Oh," answered Brunhilde. "Of course. Well, how about we give Erik a taste of your homeschool? Perhaps that will be enough to understand his school phobia."

"Right!" said Ragnar. "Ma is usually the teacher, but today, how about me? Da, can we take a break to show Erik how we do lessons?" He didn't wait for his father's response to kneel next to Erik and start measuring Erik's biceps. "Cousin, you don't look like your muscles are developed enough for math yet, so we could start with art class. First you get a big rock, see? Then you whack it as hard as you can against a different rock until it starts to look like the shape you want—"

Hrolf interrupted, "I'll help teach recess! We can try a game of Faceball to see why sports bug Erik too. We can kill two birds with one stone."

Anything called Faceball sounded like exactly the wrong way to spend the day. "Why do we have to kill any birds with any stones at all?" Erik asked. Had he actually been thinking earlier that his sister's plan was a little bit useful? Well, the useful bit was clearly going to get smothered under all the exhausting bits.

"No, no." Uncle Bjorn stopped the discussion. "Sorry,

children, we're on a schedule here. Building this must be schooling enough for now. Your mother and I can't keep sleeping with the triplets in our room forever, you know. Back to work, all of you."

The boys returned to hammering. Brunhilde walked by, and Erik clutched her ankle. He pleaded, "How about we decide that school and sports are part of the same fears as the school bus? You know, criticism and embarrassment? I promise they are about criticism and embarrassment. No need to test them. So you can take school and sports right off your list. That's good, right? You can use more of your time to box with Ragnar and stuff like that instead." He silently asked any old gods who happened to have nothing to do at the moment to make her hear him.

Brunhilde gazed at him for a long, long moment. Erik let go of her ankle. "Perhaps," she said. "But do not think we are done testing your fears, little brother. We do not go into battle against your fears without knowing all we can. We are Sheepflatteners. We do not halfway prepare for war." She pulled her notebook, folded in half, out of her back pocket and scratched a couple of notes.

Erik seized the moment to crab-walk away from her and huddle behind the triplet coop. He hoped that whatever new tests Brunhilde might plan, he'd at least have a chance to see them coming.

~

They had finished the framing, roof, and three walls when Allyson arrived in a swirl of luggage and lip gloss. "Thanks for having me, Aunt Hilda and Uncle Bjorn!" she said as Ragnar and Hrolf carried her bags and suitcases inside. "I can't wait to meet the triplets!"

Aunt Hilda beamed. "They are already so strong, Allyson. Come, have something to eat after your trip, and then we'll go over to the lake." Allyson, Brunhilde, and Erik followed their aunt into the kitchen, where she buttered a wedge of grainy bread and topped it with tiny cooked shrimp for Allyson. "Here, eat, eat!"

Hrolf came limping in with a boy triplet under each arm and Sally clutching onto his left pantleg like a blond baby sloth. Allyson squealed through her mouthful of shrimp.

"No way! Tho thweet!" She swallowed. "Give me one to cuddle!" she reached for Siegmund, who Hrolf had told Erik could be counted on to bite cuddle-seeking strangers with his one tooth. Instead, he gazed at Allyson in rapt wonder as she took him from Hrolf's arms.

"Ohhhh," he said, raising a tiny hand to pat her shiny earrings. Allyson had crafted them herself out of bits of broken Swiss Army knives, gluing together an array of tiny screwdrivers, tweezers, corkscrews, and chisels. "You like your cousin's pretty earrings? You like your pretty cousin?" She cradled Siegmund in one arm and tickled his tummy. He turned bright red and hid his face against her shirt.

Sally and Sven exchanged a glance and then looked distrustfully at Allyson. Erik knew Siegmund had cut the first tooth of the three of them, and the other babies expected him to use it. It looked like Sally and Sven were disturbed to see their fellow triplet snuggling this earring-wearing visitor without a single chomp.

Uncle Bjorn came in to hug Allyson. "How about if Hildy packs us up a picnic and we head over to the lake right now? This whole family has been working like oxen, we deserve a bit of a break to go play like bears. We can gather berries, climb trees — and shall we do some fishing, children?" he asked. Ragnar, Hrolf, and Brunhilde cheered. Erik said nothing. He hoped his more fashion-conscious sister would not want to hand-catch carnivorous fish. Maybe Allyson's visit would even delay any more phobia tests.

Allyson was now playing with Siegmund's toes and singing, "This little Viking went to market, and this little Viking stayed home, this little Viking had wild boar, and this little Viking had none . . ."

Uncle Bjorn asked her, "Are you up for fishing, Allyson?"

"You know it! Let me get changed into my new angler's outfit, and I'll be ready!"

Erik sighed.

EIGHT

THE LAKE PARK ALL-STARS

Night is dark. But dawn is always coming.
— The Lore

At the lake, Erik and Allyson helped Aunt Hilda spread out the picnic blanket while the others scoped out the best fishing site. They were at a different part of the lakeshore than where the pike had tried to swallow Erik. Here, the lake abutted a public park with a playground, splash pad, and a sloping concrete pit where skateboarders were practicing swooping around. A gathering of mountain bikers had set up an obstacle course on the far hillside and were riding their bikes over various ramps and logs. Behind them sat a large open-air amphitheater. Aunt Hilda pointed it out to Allyson.

"That's where they will hold your cheer competition tomorrow, dear," she said. "Are you ready? Has your team got any new cheers to share?"

Allyson had changed into a set of crimson waterproof hip-waders. A lesser girl might have found them hard to move around in. Not Allyson. She leapt to her feet with a gleam in her eye.

"Two, four, six, eight! Who do we eviscerate? Eight, six, four, two! This will be the end of you! GO, TEAM!" As she chanted, she performed a series of kicks and jumps that would have given a martial arts master something to worry about. She ended by crossing and lifting her forearms, where she had doodled three different runes translating to GO FIGHT WIN. "I helped write that one."

Siegmund gurgled and clapped his hands. Sally and Sven didn't.

"That's lovely, dear, just lovely." Aunt Hilda laid out platters of smoked fish, dried fish, salted fish, potatoes, rolls, and goat cheese. "Erik, can you find us a couple of rocks to hold down the ends of the blanket so they won't flutter in the breeze?"

Erik searched the ground, poking under some bushes near an older boy and a girl throwing a Frisbee back and forth. He'd found a few good-size rocks when Brunhilde came up behind him and nudged his shoulder.

Brunhilde said, "Finally, we can continue our reconnaissance. Let's go ask the Frisbee players to offer opinions and criticism of you. Hrolf made a nice checklist." She unfolded a piece of paper from her pocket with twenty-seven different things to criticize about Erik's appearance, character, habits, and intelligence.

"Nooooo," Erik moaned.

Brunhilde raised her eyebrows.

Erik thought, *Would it help if I said it louder? Or in Old Norse?* He came out with a weak *"Neinn?"*

Allyson joined them. "So, are we eating first or fishing first?"

"Neither," Brunhilde said. "We are first going to determine whether our brother has allodoxaphobia or enissophobia."

"Oh, Erik has difficulties with opinions or criticism

from other people?" Allyson tossed her hair. "Weird. Here's how to handle that, little bro." Allyson walked right up to the Frisbee-playing boy and caught the Frisbee for him. "Hi, there! Can you tell me something you don't like about me?"

"What?" the boy answered. "Uh, I don't like that you took my Frisbee without asking."

Allyson flung the Frisbee so hard it soared over the treetops and out over the lake. The boy and his friend watched it going, going . . . gone.

"Wrong answer!" Allyson sang out. "Thanks for your feedback!"

She came back over to Brunhilde and Erik. "See? Easy as cracking a bone. Any reason why we can't have lunch now?"

"Here is where things stand," Brunhilde said. "Erik is fighting a losing battle with his personal foe of fear. The cousins and I are formulating a strategy to drive his fear before him, hear the lamentations of the fear, smash his fear into tiny little fragments, and then burn those fragments into ash. So far, I have assembled this." She showed Allyson her notebook lists and sketches.

"But he is being stubborn about the tests I've designed for people phobias."

Erik felt a little proud to be called stubborn. At least it meant she noticed he was trying to AVOID her plans. He looked around Allyson at Brunhilde's notebook and saw a neat Venn diagram. Overlapping circles were labeled *EMBARRASSMENT, CRITICISM,* and *FAIL-URE* with sketches of buses, phones, pianos, and sports equipment. One circle labeled *SCIUROPHOBIA* was off to the side with a picture of a squirrel wearing armor and carrying a sharp three-pronged trident. A few other circles had drawings with question marks above them.

Allyson said, "Well, maybe you can try working on this"—she pointed to a question-marked picture of a tooth-filled fish—"if he doesn't want to deal with the people phobia stuff right now. Anyway, I'm starving, so let's go eat."

She linked arms with Brunhilde, and they walked back over to the picnic blanket, where the boys were already digging in. Erik followed behind.

"I suppose if he refuses these tests, I can label this particular enemy as both allodoxaphobia and enissophobia," Brunhilde said as they joined the picnic. Erik began to sigh with relief but immediately changed it to a cough when she frowned at him. He put the rocks he'd collected on the edges of the picnic blanket and got a plate.

Brunhilde helped herself to a scoop of potatoes and added, "At least we can move on to Erik's fear of noodling."

"Huh? I'm afraid of something called noodling?" Erik asked with his mouth full of roll.

Hrolf explained, "Oh yeah, eh? That is what the locals call the way we fish. If you catch fish by sticking your hand in a hole and pulling out whatever bites onto you, they call it noodling."

Erik swallowed. "Why don't you use fishing poles? I mean, if you catch fish with a hook on a line, then the only thing getting bitten is the worm. Your way, you are guaranteed to get bitten by something, and it could be really big and really angry."

"Yes!" yelled Hrolf. "Really big! Whoo!" He tried to high-five Erik.

"No, see, Hrolf, getting bitten by a big, angry thing

is bad because it hurts. Pain is not a good thing," Erik tried to explain.

"So you are afraid of pain." Brunhilde licked a morsel of potato off her finger and pulled *The Big Book of Fear* out of her bookbag. "That one is in the very first chapter here. It is named . . . algophobia." She made some changes to the Venn diagram. She erased two question marks and added another circle that encompassed the shark-fish and the bleeding arm and came close to overlapping the *SCIUROPHOBIA* circle. She labeled the new circle *ALGOPHOBIA (FEAR OF PAIN)*.

Erik pinched his bread roll as he watched Brunhilde write. He said, "That's not a phobia. It's normal human stuff. Pain is supposed to be your body's way of letting you know you should stop the thing you're doing and go somewhere safer."

Hrolf said, "But if you go somewhere safer, there's no fish there. Then you end up starving without any hope of catching anything. That's not smart." He forked up some fish and scratched his rune sketch, which today said BIGGER.

Uncle Bjorn chimed in. "Pain isn't a problem, Erik,

it's just something that happens when you bleed. Like Thor sends the thunder after the lightning. Besides, when you are bleeding and fishing at the same time, more big fish will come over because of the blood in the water, and that's a good thing," he finished confidently.

"Sure!" agreed Ragnar. "A feeding frenzy. It's the best!"

"What?" Erik said. "Bleeding is not the best!" He put down his half-eaten roll, his appetite gone.

"It's not a big deal — not if it helps you catch a week's worth of fish in one go," Ragnar assured him. "It's something to be very proud of. And wounds heal." He showed Erik the scars he had up and down his hands and arms. "Look at this. That's a lot of dinners. There's nothing to fear about a good meal caught for your family."

"Eating dinner is very Viking," Hrolf said. "Isn't that in the Lore?"

Erik shook his head. "Will somebody listen to me? Being afraid of blood and pain is not a phobia. It's, like, basic survival instinct. The less you bleed, the more likely you are to stay alive," he said.

Brunhilde drew another circle with an angry-looking heart pumping out spurts of angry-looking blood and wrote *HEMOPHOBIA (FEAR OF BLOOD)*.

Erik knew as deeply as he'd ever known anything that he must stay miles away from any tests his sisters and cousins might want to run to evaluate how much blood and what kind of pain he was afraid of. He grabbed Brunhilde's sparkly pen and leaned over his sister's notebook to scrawl right over the top of the two new circles, *NOT PHOBIAS, COMMON SENSE, DO NOT TEST.*

Brunhilde gave him a warning grunt. He meekly gave the pen back.

Allyson tossed her hair. "Blood is, you know, bad for clothes," she agreed. "It's very staining. Is the fear of blood like a fear of ruining your best outfits? I mean, if you were wearing a white dress, or maybe a pair of pale suede boots, blood would spell the end of them. Erik, I totes understand you."

"I don't think you do, Allyson. First off, I don't wear white dresses."

At that moment, over near the bicycle practice ramps,

one wild-haired kid ended up skidding off his bike into some gravel. He yelled, "Ow!" and one of the older riders brought over a small first aid kit.

"See?" Erik pointed at him. "That kid would agree with me. Blood and pain are not what people want out of daily life."

"Silence!" Brunhilde thundered. She looked over at the cyclists. "Those bicycle people over there can help clarify this. Shall we?" She got up and began walking over to the moaning kid with the bloody leg. Erik knew her question was an order rather than an invitation, so he joined her. Better talking to an injured cyclist than ending up in the lake covered in fish bites.

The boy who fell off his bike had soft brown eyes and a poof of wiry hair so large it was sticking out of the vents in his bike helmet. He looked about Erik's age. He was lying on the grass while a young man worked on brushing small rocks out of his wound with a moist piece of cotton. Near the grass where they knelt was a small hand-lettered sign taped to a fence post: LAKE PARK MOUNTAIN BIKE ALL-STARS TEAM (EVERYONE WELCOME).

"Fuzz," the young man said, "see if you can tap into

that daredevil spirit, but keep holding on to the handle-bars the whole time, dude-a-roni."

"I know, I know," groaned Fuzz. "Ride the bike, don't let it ride you." He looked over the young man's shoulder at Brunhilde and Erik. "Uh, hi?"

The young man turned around to see who the kid he called Fuzz was greeting. "Hey, there, newbies, come to join the practice? Helmets are mandatory. We have some extras over there, plus kneepads and elbow pads."

"Thank you for the invitation," Brunhilde said, "but we are here to settle a disagreement." She addressed the boy, "Bleeding bicyclist, my brother believes most peo-ple actively avoid pain and bleeding because it is human nature. The rest of our family thinks feeling upset about pain and bleeding is the telltale sign of a phobia. What is your opinion?"

The boy Fuzz winced slightly as the man who had rinsed his wound and dried it was now securing a very large Band-Aid over the area. "Uhhhh . . . are you ask-ing me if I am afraid of hurting myself and bleeding?"

Brunhilde nodded. "Yes. Is it normal to you?"

Fuzz pushed himself upright and tested out his leg.

He grimaced slightly but then smiled at his first aid helper. "It's good, Coach Gary. I'll get back on for my next turn." He looked at Brunhilde and Erik. "I don't like getting hurt during practice, but I like trying new moves. The first thing Coach told us when we joined was that we could get hurt, but the better we listen and follow the rules, the less that will happen. I mean, I usually end up getting hurt just walking around my house and stuff. My ma says I get my clumsiness from her side of the family. So . . . I guess I don't want to end up bloody, but I'm not gonna let it stop me from having fun."

Coach Gary put away the bandages and ointment in his red first aid pack. "Pretty much not a practice goes by without somebody eating a little dirt or getting a few scratches," he admitted. "That's why we wear safety equipment, and my first priority is teaching everyone how to prevent serious harm. But no matter how many Band-Aids we have to use, we call it a good day if we're smiling at the end of it!" He did a complicated handshake with Fuzz and told him to get back in the line of kids who were continuing to pedal through the obstacle course.

The young coach offered his hand to Erik to shake. "I'm Gary Tischer, the leader of this gang. It's a multi-age mountain bike team, just started this year. Most of these kids have never ridden before, so we're getting into the basics." He gave Erik a calculating look. "Say, are you around fourth or fifth grade? We've got room in the nine-to-eleven-year-old category if you want to get in line behind Fuzz."

"Yeah!" Fuzz grinned as he lifted his bandaged leg over his bike frame. "We're going to do speed drills next. They're my favorite! By the way, I'm Fuzz. My mom hates when I tell people that, because she thinks Fahid is a perfectly good name, but I can't help that I'm a fuzzy kind of guy."

Erik was at a loss for words. He knew how to ride a bike. But this was an organized sports team, and those never worked out well for him, so of course he should say no. Still, there was something about the way Fuzz was smiling and offering him the helmet, like it was a golden ticket to a happy place.

"Huh," he said.

Brunhilde narrowed her eyes at him. "Pardon us for

a moment, please," she said to Coach Gary and Fuzz. She pulled him to the side.

"Are you considering being part of this group? It might be a very good strategy." She looked over the gathering of boys and girls. They were laughing together, trying to balance on their bikes with both feet on the pedals and then falling over in the grass in slow motion. "There appears to be a wealth of opportunities for embarrassment, failure, and bloody injuries. I bet we could get them to criticize you after every practice. Also, if I am not mistaken, I see a squirrel nest in that tree right there."

Erik had been half-listening until the word *squirrel,* at which point he shook his head emphatically. "N-n-n-n-no thanks," he stuttered to Fuzz and backed away. "I don't think it's my kind of thing."

Brunhilde grunted and said, "Thank you for talking to us, Fuzz of the Bloody Leg and Coach Gary of the First Aid Kit. May you have an afternoon with as much or as little pain as you see fit." She and Erik returned to the picnic blanket.

~

Erik watched the rest of the family splashing around in the lake. Sally sat in his lap. He'd clued in to the fact that offering to watch the triplets was like a get-out-of-jail-free card: no one would ask him to do any other task if he was taking care of all three babies. Sven and Siegmund were napping, so currently he had to make sure Sally didn't wiggle-crawl off by herself. Brunhilde had frowned when he wouldn't try noodling, but even she could not argue with him handling full triplet diaper duty.

"Fish, like, on!" Allyson yelled. He saw Allyson waving one wet hand with a bass glorped onto it. Aunt Hilda high-fived her other hand. Ragnar kept sticking his legs under a mini island of branches and debris and kicking his feet out of the water, punting scaly things over to Hrolf and Uncle Bjorn. Brunhilde was stuffing perch in her pockets. Erik watched their splashing and wished there was a smaller gap between so many of the things his family liked to do and the things he felt comfortable doing.

Erik felt Sally's gums grab his arm and yelped. The little girl started sucking on his forearm like he was a tasty teething toy. She could down a bottle quicker than either of her brothers, and now he knew why — she had some powerful suction. He let her slurp away for a little while until he started to worry she might actually flay the top layer of his skin right off. It wasn't easy to get a finger between her lips and his arm to break the seal, but eventually he popped her mouth free, leaving a big red-and-pink welt.

Sally and Erik regarded the welt together. It looked a lot like Brunhilde's drawing of the angry-looking heart pumping out spurts of angry-looking blood for hemophobia. It also looked uncannily like the Old Norse rune for DISASTER.

"What are you doing, Sally, trying to give me a rune tattoo?" he asked her. "It's like the whole family is in on this together. Doesn't anyone else see that AVOIDING STUFF is a good plan?"

Sally replied by grunting, leaning forward, and slurping some more.

NINE

DRAGON BREATHING

When the biggest tree needs
felling, take it one chop at a time.
— The Lore

Allyson was up early the next day, frying a pan filled with a half dozen eggs, four shredded potatoes, and six slices of bacon as Erik and his cousins wandered in to the kitchen.

"Yum," said Hrolf. "I'll take a plate of that."

"Then you'll have to cook some yourself," she said primly, sliding the entire contents of the pan into a big bowl. "This is for me. It's cheer competition day, and I need to keep my energy up."

Aunt Hilda and Uncle Bjorn joined them. Aunt Hilda told the boys to round up some more food from the larder and gather the morning's eggs from their chickens so everyone could have a big breakfast. She then sat at the table with a sigh and began reminiscing. "We had something like cheer camp back in Norway, you know. It was called the Svalbard Skrik. I won two years in a row," she said.

"Oh yeah, eh, when I met her, your mother's voice could peel the bark off an ironwood tree," Uncle Bjorn agreed, and sipped his mug of coffee. Hilda blushed, and they held hands, smiling at each other.

Erik watched Allyson continue to shovel down her mound of food. When she was nearly done, Brunhilde slid into the chair next to Erik. Her eyes were tired.

"You had better eat a good breakfast too, Erik," she said. "Ragnar and I were up late discussing how to begin the War on Fear. He enjoys planning battle strategies almost as much as I do." She looked at Allyson and scowled. "What is that on your arm?"

Allyson glanced down as she shoveled in her last big mouthful. "Mm-hmm, like it?" she asked indistinctly.

She'd given herself a temporary tattoo of a bunny labeled SWEET PRINCESS, and below it she had sketched the rune for CONQUER.

"Conquer is my rune," growled Brunhilde.

Allyson finished and cleared her place. "Well, I'm feeling conquery today, Bru! You don't own all the conquering!" She tossed her hair from side to side and flounced out of the kitchen to go get changed.

Ragnar looked at his own arm. "You are lucky, Brunhilde. You found your rune early. I just don't know what to do." He showed them that he had changed his tattoo from SMASH back to CRUSH. "Crush . . . or smash? Smash . . . or crush? It's so hard to be me."

Brunhilde grunted and turned back to Erik. "Since you are resisting any more tests and reconnaissance, I believe it is time to move on to the next phase: the initial skirmish. We have enough information to prepare for your first battle today."

Erik's mouth had been watering over the idea of a big plate of bacony goodness, but now it went dry. "What do you mean by prepare for battle?" he asked. After he said it, his stomach felt like it was considering climbing out of his belly button and skittering off somewhere to hide. Was Brunhilde going to try opening him up to locate where his fears began and pluck them out? Was Ragnar going to try brain surgery with a battle-axe?

Brunhilde yawned and then began working her way around a plate of bread and honey. "Things are more complicated than I had originally thought. While we can now see that your enemies are predictable, you appear to have no active defense against them. And the things Ragnar and I know about defensive moves in hand-to-hand combat do not apply here."

"Yeah, but do my defensive moves smash things more? Or crush them more?" Ragnar interjected. "Hey . . . is *crush-smash* a word?"

Brunhilde ignored him. "Fighting invisible things like feelings, well, that demands a whole new way of thinking. The last chapter in *The Big Book of Fear* offered some ideas. So did *The Art of War*. But it took a fair amount of puzzling out." She yawned again, showing a mouthful of half-chewed bread. "I will show you."

And after they ate (Erik managed to nibble on a

couple slices of bacon; the smell of crisp, smoky bacon can usually tempt even the unhappiest stomach), she did.

In the playroom, Brunhilde and Ragnar had laid out a large piece of paper on top of a coffee table and drawn a landscape labeled *ERIK VS. EVERYTHING*. Brunhilde had used some of Hrolf's tin soldiers and army men and a few of the triplets' toys and stuffed animals to represent Erik's various fears. She had also borrowed carved pieces from Uncle Bjorn's personal Hnefatafl set, an archaic Norse game known as Fist Chess.

"Whoa." Erik examined the landscape. Brunhilde had obviously put a lot of work into it. Seeing his fears laid out systematically like this was impressive. For instance, in the Foothills of Embarrassment, she had a phalanx of twenty fighters with a toy bus, and in the blue-construction-paper Sea of Squirrels, she'd set a battleship mounted by a giant stuffed squirrel with a butter knife taped to its paws. It was like a game board for a demented version of Mouse Trap.

Hrolf started rolling a tank through the Plains of

Failure toward the Castle of Criticism. Ragnar pretended to counterattack the tank with a platoon of soldiers operating the Cannon of Piano Lessons.

"What's that?" Erik asked. He pointed to the top of an overturned brown measuring cup.

"That's us," Brunhilde answered.

Atop the measuring cup she had placed a small walnut surrounded by four painted figurines from the Hnefatafl set. One figurine was a helmeted Valkyrie, two were fur-clad barbarians holding enormous swords, and one was a princess in a flowing gown with a fencing saber.

"What's the little walnut for?" Erik asked.

"You're the walnut," said Ragnar. He pointed to the bigger barbarian. "That's me, of course. We're up on the high ground because that's all we have going for us right now. Our one advantage is that we can see the enemies around us."

"Why am I a walnut?" Erik asked. He was the smallest, least-impressive looking item on the whole board.

"Because you would taste good cooked in pancakes?"

Ragnar guessed. "Ask your sister, she figured that one out."

Brunhilde rubbed her forehead. "I thought about this a lot last night. I have been taking notes on every fear we have tested. I have watched your reactions so carefully. And while it is disheartening that you never fight back as most Sheepflatteners would, you also manage to . . . survive." She looked into his eyes. "Nine years of fighting all this" — she swept her hand to indicate the whole board — "and you are still here. You must have a thick shell. And since you are a member of this family, I know that inside that shell must be the nutmeat of greatness, which, once planted in the proper soil, will burst forth and grow into a mighty tree —"

Just then, a curious wiggling Sally nudged open the bedroom door. Right behind her, Mr. Nubbins scampered in, his bright black eyes surveying the room. In a flash, he was up on the table, scattering army men and kicking the stuffed butter-knife-wielding squirrel in the head. He leapt onto the measuring cup, grabbed the walnut, chittered at Erik, and was gone. Erik, almost as quick as Mr. Nubbins, dove under the coffee table with a shriek.

Brunhilde didn't miss a beat. She scooped up the fallen Hnefatafl figures and replaced them in the circle. She pulled another walnut out of her pocket and replaced it in the center of the measuring cup. She continued her speech. "As I was saying, you will burst forth and grow into a mighty tree —"

Mr. Nubbins appeared again in a flash of fur. He rushed the measuring cup like a tiny gray tornado, successfully nabbed the second walnut, and disappeared out the door. Brunhilde closed the door, growled, and cast about herself for a something to replace the captured nuts. She plucked a tiny wooden turtle from the triplets' zoo set and put it on the measuring cup. Then she grabbed Erik's arm and hauled him out from under the coffee table.

She said, "You, with your thick shell, may be much like a nut, or much like a turtle, Erik, son of Inge and Thorfast, brother of mine. A small, seemingly powerless turtle. A small, seemingly powerless, unimpressive turtle. A small, powerless, unimpressive turtle that will not even try to swim if the waves are too big—"

"I get it, Bru, I get it." Erik used his shirtsleeve to wipe away the squirrel-induced sweat from his forehead.

She clasped his arm. "But your shell is as thick as a Viking sword is sharp. We will use that. And we will win."

Erik continued wiping his face and studied the strategy board. As weird as it looked, the environment his sister had constructed seemed very familiar. It really did resemble the way the world felt to him whenever he crawled out from under his bed. A world filled with potential fears, ready to strike.

Then he looked at the turtle on the plastic cup surrounded by warrior figures. And he surprised himself and his sister by giving her quick one-armed hug.

~

A few minutes later, Allyson, who had changed into her cheer outfit, came into the bedroom with pompoms at the ready. "What are you up to?" she asked. "We're leaving in, like, forty-five minutes."

Brunhilde paged intently through *The Big Book of Fear*. She had already explained to the boys and a wide-eyed, thumb-sucking Sally how the *ERIK VS. EVERY-THING* map had been set up. She was now rereading the final chapter in *The Big Book*. "Hello, Allyson. We were going to practice our first strike against Erik's enemies. I want to get this right, so we have to work together on it."

"Right," Allyson agreed brightly. "Where are our weapons?"

"Well," Brunhilde said, and paused. "Here." She pointed to a circle of comfy pillows.

"What, are they under the pillows?"

"They are the pillows. As I was telling Erik, I have thought about this a lot. Sun Tzu writes *Attack where the enemy is unprepared*. All Erik's fears have ever known is for him to freak out and run away. So doing anything to stop the fears will be unexpected. And how does one attack a fear? I read the afterword of *The Big Book* last night, and it mentions two ideas. One of them is called exposure therapy. It is where one exhausts one's fears by being exposed to them with no escape, like forcing someone with elevator phobia to ride up and down in an elevator for hours. Or forcing someone with spider phobia to ride up and down in a spider-filled elevator for hours. Eventually, their body gets tired and their fear gives up."

Erik's legs went weak, and he waved his arms. "The other one," he gulped. "Whatever the other way is, let's practice that one. Not exposure therapy. Please."

"Yes," Brunhilde agreed, "that was my plan. The other thing is much simpler to arrange. It involves breathing techniques." She paused and skeptically sucked her lower lip.

Hrolf snorted and asked, "How are we gonna smash anything with breathing techniques?"

Brunhilde shrugged. "This is new ground for me too, little cousin," she answered. "Perhaps we can envision this as a sneak attack." She pulled some cotton balls out of a box and arranged them on the game board around the Hnefatafl figures. She looked at it critically and then put one more cotton ball on top of the turtle for good measure. "Think of the cotton balls as our breathing. When fears hit them, they are supposed to become immobilized, powerless. Perhaps they even dissolve."

Ragnar nodded. "Maybe it's like chemical warfare, like tear gas. Or maybe it's like we have wizardry on our side, like our breath becomes a devastating magic mist."

Hrolf yelled, "Our breath can dissolve enemies?" He slapped his hand down on the floor. "I get it! We're like dragons! Cool! I want to learn Dragon Breath."

Brunhilde looked both uncomfortable and resolute. "Anyway, there is a short training regimen outlined on this page on how to make our breathing a powerful source of protection against fears. We will practice it together to support Erik. Are you doing this with us, Allyson?"

"Well, sure I am! Breathing techniques are good for controlling cheer volume. What's not to love? Let's be conquery. GO, TEAM!" Allyson shook her pompoms.

Erik said, "I'll try the pillow thing if you promise not to do the elevator-full-of-spiders thing."

Brunhilde nodded. "Let us start the drill. Battle stations!" she ordered. Ragnar, Hrolf, and Allyson moved to occupy one comfy pillow apiece in the circle. Hrolf made a spot for Sally next to him on a knitted blanket. Erik sat on a pillow embroidered with the Sheepflattener family crest: a red and blue shield with two axes crossed over a deflated-looking sheep.

Brunhilde stayed standing outside the circle, holding *The Big Book of Fear*. "Cross your legs! Sit up straight! Hands open on your knees!" she barked. She walked behind Hrolf. "Hands OPEN, I said. Put down the cookie."

She opened up the book and began to recite the relaxation directions. "Now. Notice your breath. Feel it. Hear it. Concentrate. There is nothing else. No room, no me, no fears, no pillow, just your breath. Concentrate. Breathe in. Breathe out." She strode around the circle as she talked. As she walked behind Erik, she paused and then smacked him on the back of the head.

"Ow! What was that for?"

"Concentrate."

"I *am* concentrating."

She smacked the back of his head again. "Concentrate so hard you don't notice me smacking the back of your head. I said there is no me." She continued reading. "Now. Think these exact words: *Breathe in, I see myself as a mountain. Breathe out, I feel solid.* In: mountain. Out: solid. *Breathing in, I am a deep pool of water. Breathing out, my surface is still.* In: water. Out: still."

Erik did as Brunhilde said. He felt his breath running up through his throat and out of his nose. *In, water. Out, still.* He imagined himself a small snowcapped mountain. He imagined he was a stream running down the mountain into a deep icy-blue pool. *In. Out.* This wasn't so bad, yet.

Hrolf slumped to the ground to tickle Sally's tummy. "Relaxation makes me hungry."

Brunhilde grabbed the back of Hrolf's shirt and hauled him back onto his pillow. "Legs crossed, back straight," she said. "War is hell, little cousin. You will have to be hungry for a while longer yet. Now comes the hard part." She took a seat on the last pillow and cleared her throat. "Now we close our eyes and sit in silence."

The others closed their eyes and sat.

"Sorry, wait, there cannot yet be silence because I need to explain the silence," Brunhilde said as she read the final paragraph in *The Big Book*. "Do not think about anything. You are here to breathe, not to think, not to plan, not to worry, not to judge. Do not think about food, Hrolf." Hrolf groaned softly. "Do not think about Mr. Nubbins cracking you open like a walnut, Erik." Erik could now think of nothing else. "When thoughts arise, bring your attention back to your breath." She closed the book. "That is what the directions say. So we do it." Then she slammed the book on the floor and roared, "Do it! Breathe like you mean it! Breathe like Erik's freedom depends on it!"

Erik worked on breathing like he meant it. Shaking his head, he tried to push away the image of a huge squirrel nibbling him open to get at his tasty insides.

Next to him, Ragnar made a gentle snorting sound. Erik's eyelids popped open. Allyson was smiling as she sat. Hrolf was holding a wooden toy dog in front of his mouth, puffing and blowing on it, probably hoping he'd transform into a fire-breathing dragon-boy. Ragnar was drooling slightly with an open mouth. Erik's eyes next met Brunhilde's, who stabbed a finger at him and mouthed, *Concentrate*. He immediately scrunched his eyes shut again. His breathing was shallow and quick. He tried to pay attention to it rushing in and out against the little hairs inside his nose.

In, out. In, out. In . . . out. He noticed that his lungs went right along sucking air in and pushing it out without his having to tell them to do anything. *Look at 'em go,* he thought. *At least my lungs seem to get what we're supposed to be doing here.* After about ten minutes, against all his natural tendencies, Erik relaxed. When Uncle Bjorn knocked on the playroom door and stuck his head inside, Erik didn't even move except to crack open his eyelids.

"Time to head over for the competition, everyone. Don't want to Allyson to be late. Go, team!" he said, and did a little kicking dance step. He took another look at the children in the pillow circle. "What are you doing, then, praying to the old gods?"

Hrolf finished his cookie in two bites and dashed to his father. "We're learning Dragon Breathing, Da! To smite our enemies!"

Uncle Bjorn rubbed Hrolf's head. "Are you, now?

Always good to learn a new way to smite things, son. Now, bring Sally, and let's get a move on."

One of Erik's legs had gone to sleep, and he had trouble extracting it from the crisscross sitting position. Brunhilde walked over and helped pull him upright. "So, turtle brother, what did you think of our first strategy session?" she asked.

Erik rubbed his pins-and-needles leg. Despite Mr. Nubbins's earlier appearance, his insides weren't particularly full of fear shards. "I think that it wouldn't hurt to do it again," he said, trying to not let on that he was kind of excited. Brunhilde's mad methods might have unearthed one good idea.

Allyson bounced over and grabbed Brunhilde's arm, yanking her out the door. "Come on, being relaxed doesn't mean being slow! I want you to get good seats for the competition. Let's go!"

TEN

ERIK THE VIKING GOES MOUNTAIN BIKING

We will find a way or we will make one.
— Hannibal, military commander, 218 BC
(adopted as part of the Lore)

The amphitheater was already getting crowded by the time the Sheepflatteners arrived. Allyson ran over to her teammates to begin warming up. Teenage boys and girls in cheer uniforms stretched their legs in painful-looking splits on the grass. One team nearby wore uniforms with the word WYVERNS stitched across the front in flame-shaped letters. Hrolf nudged Erik.

"Wyverns are dragons, you know, a kind that walks

to two legs. I betcha they practice Dragon Breathing like us," Hrolf said.

Erik and Hrolf watched as the Wyvern team gathered in a circle, linking arms. They recited in a rhythmic chant, bobbing their heads up and down, "We can DO this CHEER, uh-huh. We will FACE our FEAR, what what? Fear just makes us YAWN—hoo-WAH. Soon it will be GONE, oh yeah. Only we will remain. ONLY WE WILL REMAIN! Gooooooo, WYVERNS!" They unlinked arms and finished the chant with a flailing free-for-all.

"Did you hear that?" Erik said to Brunhilde on his left and Hrolf on his right. "They were talking about dealing with fear."

Hrolf was trying to signal a peanut seller to come over to their row. "Yeah, dealing with deer is cool. I'd do cheer camp too if you could hunt deer while you cheer."

"Not deer, *fear*. Did you hear them, Brunhilde?" Erik said.

Brunhilde was deep in a discussion with Ragnar about the design of the amphitheater and how it resembled Roman sites of gladiatorial combat. She waved

137

toward Hrolf and said, "Yes, what he said. I like deer, too."

"Not deer, *fear*. Forget it." Erik went back to watching the cheer teams warm up. There were more than fifty different teams from the Northeast and Midwest. Most seemed to be named after animals, both the mythological like the Winchester Wyverns and the Menomonie Minotaurs, and the more ordinary like the Holyoke Hedgehogs and the Caledonia Cuddly Kittens. Despite the crowds, Allyson's home team was easy to spot among the competitors. All of Ridgewell's sports teams carried the same name, the Ridgewell Ridgebacks, named for an intimidating African dog breed with a ridge of spiky fur running along its spine. Allyson's cheer team had yellow uniforms with stiff brown bristles running along their backs. As they practiced getting ready, the Ridgeback team encouraged one another by barking and howling.

Aunt Hilda pointed them out to her boys. "Allyson told me she came up with the idea of showing their teeth like that," she said. "Oh, this is so exciting! I'd love to be down there yowling with them!"

The judges soon got the competition underway. Erik

enjoyed watching the teenagers jump around and fling each other in the air. The Hedgehogs were a crowd favorite, displaying an unusual move where they rolled up into little balls and swirled around the grass in a syn-chronized sort of bowling-ball ballet. The Wyverns were amazing, launching into the air so high they almost seemed to fly.

However, no one could touch the Ridgebacks. Even Erik, who had not a clue as to what earned a team points, could see they were head and shoulders above the rest. Literally. Half the girls on the team carried another girl on their shoulders throughout the routine, performing martial-arts-inspired jumps like the ones Allyson had demonstrated back at their uncle and aunt's house. They were like super-cheerful double-decker ninjas, huge grins on their faces while they hurled themselves from one side of the amphitheater to the other. Erik stood up with his family to applaud when their routine came to a growling, howling finish. Aunt Hilda held Siegmund above her head as he squeaked.

Allyson, sweating hard under the weight of her team-mate, beamed at the crowd. It was no surprise to anyone at the end of the competition when the Ridgebacks were awarded first place.

When Allyson came over to receive hugs from Aunt Hilda and Uncle Bjorn, she asked, "What did you think of the eviscerate cheer? Did you like it? Remember, that one was mine!"

"Never seen a better evisceration, angel," Uncle Bjorn said. "Your family and your ancestors are both proud of you this day. Why don't we go out to celebrate at the Pie Slab?" The Pie Slab was a restaurant in town that served enormous pies, both sweet and savory. About a week ago, Erik had helped Ragnar deliver a crate of meat after Uncle Bjorn had trapped more wild boar than the family could use.

"Can I go home to change first?" Allyson asked. "Wouldn't want to get any pie on my uniform."

Aunt Hilda said, "Of course, let's head home to clean up. Then we'll go eat and share stories of Viking triumphs past." She began to lead the way out of the amphitheater, but had to suddenly jump back to escape being run over by a mountain biker out of control.

"Whoa, whoa, SO sorry!" the mountain biker yelled as he passed and crashed into a tree, somersaulting over his handlebars, then landing in a tuck and rolling safely to a stop, unharmed. It was Fuzz, the boy with the scraped-up leg they'd met earlier that week. Riding right behind him was Gary, the coach.

"Fuzz, what did I say about the bike riding you?" Coach Gary called out. He stopped in front of Aunt Hilda. "Ma'am, are you all right? Fuzz is a little bit of a hazard to himself and others. He's still learning."

Aunt Hilda said, "Kids will be kids, won't they? No harm done, young man, thank you for checking."

A tall teenager followed after Coach Gary, skidding his bike sideways with a crunching hiss that sprayed gravel on Erik. He came to a stop in front of Brunhilde and Allyson and pulled off his helmet to display strong cheekbones and tousled black hair. He looked Allyson up and down in her uniform and jutted out his chin in greeting. "'Sup," he said.

Allyson burst into uncontrolled giggles. "Wow, you are so good at riding that thing! You must be, like, a mountain bike champion!" Brunhilde looked at her sister as if she might have gotten some form of brain damage during the cheer competition.

"Yeah," the tall boy answered, tossing his hair off his forehead. "That's me. I'm, like, a mountain bike champion. Name's Dylan."

Allyson giggled some more. "I'm Allyson. I'm on the team that just won the cheer competition!"

The boy nodded. "Winning stuff is cool. Want to stay and watch me practice?"

Brunhilde broke into the conversation. "No time right now. We need to head home with our family." She draped an arm around Allyson's shoulders and pushed her toward the path to the house. Dylan shrugged and put his helmet back on, spinning his wheels to produce a new shower of gravel and pumping his pedals back up the hill. Allyson turned to watch him go and sighed. Brunhilde tightened her grip on her twin and continued leading her away.

Coach Gary had gathered up Fuzz and his bicycle and made sure nothing was broken on either boy or bike. They were preparing to ride back up the hill as well.

Fuzz patted Erik's arm as he walked by. "Hey, I remember you! You're the kid who thinks bleeding is bad. Or good. Or messy? I forget which. But listen, today we lost one of the riders in our age group. His mom made him go to violin lessons instead, so we need another rider to join our team. You want to do it, right? Did I tell you how much fun it is?"

"That's true," Coach Gary joined in. "We are looking for another rider in the upper-elementary group, and you're exactly the right size for the bike we have. Why don't you come give it a try, at least? You might like it."

Erik started to mumble a polite excuse when he saw Brunhilde turn around to look for him. She said something to Ragnar, and he took Allyson's arm as Brunhilde trotted back to join her brother.

"Please do not start giggling at mountain bike riders too, Erik," she warned. "Come, we must prepare for pie."

Coach Gary stuck out his hand. "I don't think we have been properly introduced. I'm Gary, and you are . . ."

"Brunhilde," she answered, gripping his hand so hard Coach Gary winced a bit. "Daughter of Inge and

Thorfast, granddaughter of Golveg and Vigdis, sister of Allyson and Erik."

"Okay, then," Coach Gary answered. "Well, we just invited your brother here to join us in practicing some mountain bike skills. Our team really needs another rider since we had someone quit. We can only get funding for our program if we have at least nine riders, one for each sponsored bike. Can you spare him for the afternoon so he can see if he wants to join? I promise we'll take good care of him."

Brunhilde said to Erik, "No time today, brother. After celebrating Allyson's victory, I was planning to get your exposure therapy training set up. Ragnar and I had an idea of how we can fit you and Mr. Nubbins plus a ringing phone into the same small cage—"

"I'll do it," Erik said to Coach Gary and Fuzz. "I'll come mountain bike."

"Great!" Coach Gary said. "Follow us, and we'll outfit you with some gear. It's a blast."

Erik looked up into Brunhilde's face with what defiance he could muster, expecting to see specks of fury burning in her eyes at having her exposure therapy plans thwarted. Instead, she winked and chased after the rest of the family.

Erik blinked in astonishment. What would make Brunhilde wink? Nope, he decided, he didn't want to know.

He followed the cyclists up the hill.

~

At the top of the slope, the mountain bike team-in-training had gathered around the large trunk of a fallen tree. It was almost waist-high to the tallest kid. Plywood planks had been placed on either side, forming ramps. Strapping on a helmet, Erik watched the other kids taking turns attempting to ride up a plank, balance on the trunk, and ride down the other side. A few of the taller kids made it from one side to the other to many admiring shouts. Other kids started pedaling up the ramp but then stopped short and hopped off. The team called out words of encouragement for every attempt.

"Go, Funmi, go, you can do it, you can do it . . . Okay, you can't do it, but you looked good trying!" someone yelled at a girl who turned back before she even tried going up the ramp.

"Who's up next? Lily, give it a shot! Get up some speed! Wait, not that much speed! Are you okay, Lily? She's — she's okay, she's one tough girl!"

"Leo, Leo, Leo, he's gonna shred this, here he goes, here he . . . doesn't go! Okay, he'll get it next time!" Coach Gary said to a boy who gamely shot up the ramp and then slid sideways off the tree trunk. "All right, gang, huddle up, I want to introduce you to our newest recruit." He motioned Erik over. "As you know, we lost Juan to the dreaded world of violin lessons." Everyone booed. "But this fine young man has agreed to try taking over his spot. Let's give a warm welcome to Erik!"

Everyone recited in a bored singsongy voice as if they were in a classroom, "A warm welcome to Erik." Then they broke into big smiles and surrounded Erik, individually shaking his hand or waving to introduce themselves.

"Hi, I'm Lily, I'm kinda terrible at this, but I love it."

"Yo, Erik, I'm Derek, we should form a band or something, because we rhyme."

"Hi. Dylan. 'Sup."

"I'm Leo, and this is my sister Morgan, we did some mountain biking last year so we can explain anything that doesn't make sense. Do you have any experience?" one boy asked Erik.

"Uh . . . no. I mean, I've ridden a regular bike, but I've never even seen a mountain bike before now," Erik confessed. Coach Gary wheeled over a knobby-tired bike decorated with stickers of people's heads. It had accordion-like shock absorbers under the seat and on the front fork. He pushed it to Erik, who put his hands gingerly on the handlebars.

"Well, have you ever gotten a haircut?" asked Leo's sister Morgan. She wore an orange headscarf under her helmet.

"Yes," Erik answered. "But never because I wanted to." He didn't much like having scissors near his head. Plus, he'd always agreed with the bit of the Lore that stated *Those longer of hair are stronger and fairer.* "Why?"

"Well, maybe you'd want to get it cut if you earned it. Your bike's sponsored by the Hair Shack. Anyone who rides it gets a free trim after a race, doesn't even matter whether you whether you win or not," Morgan answered. "My bike is from the animal shelter, so I can go in and play with kittens and puppies and hamsters. Leo gets to mail a free letter at the post office." Leo's bike was covered in canceled stamps.

"That's right," Coach Gary added. "Our team is sort of an experiment this year, where a group of local business owners agreed to sponsor bikes so any kid could join and ride. Alice Toeclips at the post office is a big mountain biking advocate, and she convinced other folks that they'd get good publicity by advertising on our bikes. You don't mind being our Hair Shack Hero, do you?" Erik shrugged. "Okay, everyone, back to practicing. I'm going to show Erik how to handle this baby and how to fall off without losing any of his teeth. Because what do we know?"

The kids recited in a chorus, "Falling doesn't have to mean getting hurt. Safety first, fun second!" except for Dylan, who chanted, "Winning first, winning second!" Everyone else ignored Dylan, and the group got back to practicing.

Just like that, Erik became a member of the Lake Park All-Stars Mountain Bike Team (Everyone Welcome). Coach Gary gave him a basic startup lesson, and he spent the rest of the afternoon mostly watching his new teammates try to master the tree trunk. Erik tried out his bike when no one was looking at him. The knobby tires on the Hair Shack–sponsored bike gripped the ground, and its frame was pretty heavy, so even if Erik pushed the pedals hard, he didn't move very fast. He listened to Coach Gary explain how obstacles were easier to bike over, under, and around when riders "made friends with gravity." Erik had started furtively trying out a move called a bunny hop when Ragnar came jogging up to him.

"Erik! I bring news!" Ragnar said.

Erik was standing on the pedals, leaning back, but when Ragnar spoke, he mistimed pulling up his back wheel and . . . whoops. But Erik tucked and rolled like Coach Gary taught him to and came up unscathed.

"What news? What is it?" Erik asked his cousin.

Ragnar's face was solemn. "I looked it up in the dictionary. *Crush-smash* is not a word."

Erik waited to see if Ragnar had any other news to add to this revelation.

"You know when you mean to crush something, but then you accidentally smash it instead? There ought to be a word for that."

Erik said, "I don't think the dictionary understands your problems." Ragnar wagged his head in dismayed agreement. Erik knew how being misunderstood felt and wished he could help, so he offered some uplifting Lore-style advice. *"Make plenty of time to hear stories and eat corn exploded over the fire. Skimp not on the butter and salt, and happiness shall be yours."*

Ragnar looked thoughtful. "Hey, that reminds me —I also came to tell you that everyone's over at the Pie Slab now if you want to come and eat with us," he said.

Coach Gary looked at his watch. "Right, that's all the time we have for today, gang," he said to the team. "You know the drill: leave the bikes, pads, and brain buckets with me. Same time, same station this Wednesday." The team began to disperse. "Thanks for giving us a try, Erik. So what do you say—want to train with us for next few weeks? It's free, and we meet three afternoons a week right here." He recited the days and times. "July twenty-seventh, there's a big downhill race through the woods over there," he pointed to the far side of the park. "Anyone who trains can enter the race. In fact, I had to promise Alice from the post office that every sponsored bike would be in the race. First prize is a ham."

Erik undid his helmet strap. Ham was good, but not as important as what had just happened. He had just spent the past forty minutes around a group of people who seemed to think that everything he was doing or not doing was just fine. He had learned how to fall off a bike and roll to safety. Nothing really scary or awful had happened. This was probably the closest he could get to hiding under a bed in his current situation.

"I think I do want to come back," he said.

"Yes!" yelled Fuzz. "Told you it was fun. Next time, I'll show you how to do this." He tried to do a wheelie and flipped the whole bike over onto himself. "I'm okay," he gasped. Coach Gary pulled Fuzz's bike, covered with stickers of flowers and vegetables (sponsored by the local garden shop with a free packet of seeds for its rider after a race), off him. "I'm okay."

Erik smiled and helped Fuzz to his feet. "How about next time you show me more falling-down-without-getting-hurt skills instead?"

"You got it! We are going to crush the under-eleven category in the race, I just know it." Fuzz waved and ran off to meet his mom, while Ragnar and Erik headed for the Pie Slab, Ragnar continuing to explore how to weigh the value of crushing against the appeal of smashing. Erik didn't have any more advice to share, but did his best to be a good listener.

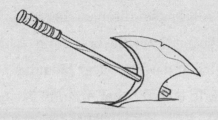

ELEVEN

DODGING EXPOSURE THERAPY

Wear the best possible socks, and
any weather can be braved.
— The Lore

The Monday following the cheer competition, Brunhilde gathered the cousins after breakfast to practice what Hrolf insisted on calling Dragon Breathing.
"We are going to practice this until we master it," she
told them. "Every morning, you sit here on these pillows
or you'll have me to answer to."

No one complained. In fact, by the end of the second practice, Hrolf drew a stumpy-looking dragon on

his forearm, Allyson said it made her lungs happy, and Ragnar said he might try the breathing technique when out bow-fishing at dawn to clear his mind and still his arrow. And Erik thought that *breathe like you mean it* was some of the best advice he'd ever heard. He could be calm the whole time he sat on that pillow.

Tuesday morning, he was so entranced with the air going in and out of his lungs, he didn't notice until Brunhilde instructed them to open their eyes that Sally had wiggle-crawled into his lap. He blinked at the baby snoozing across his crossed legs like a cat. Being calm enough for a baby to fall asleep on him made Erik feel strong and protective. Sally eventually opened her eyes and smiled up at him. He saw that she had the beginnings of her own tooth poking through her lower gums.

"Pretty soon you won't have to rely on Siegmund to bite people for you anymore," he said. She gurgled.

Wednesday morning didn't go quite so well.

Erik opened his eyes at the end of breathing practice and found this time, baby Sven sat nestled upright atop his crossed legs. He reached out a hand to smooth his cousin's downy hair. His hand froze when he realized Sven held something on his own little lap: Mr. Nubbins. Sven was sucking on the squirrel's good ear.

All of Erik's relaxation went right out the window. "Get it off me!" Erik choked out.

Brunhilde cocked her head to the side. "Very good," she finally said. "You are now trapped with one of your phobias. I believe this can count as exposure therapy." She found the proper page in *The Big Book* and scanned the instructions. "Okay, Erik, here is what you need to do: Continue sitting there. Continue falling apart. You will eventually become too exhausted to be afraid. If you can survive to exhaustion, the power sciurophobia has over you will be broken."

"If I can survive? IF?" Erik couldn't take his eyes off the little gray body. That furry tail was going to twitch any second. He knew it. His entire nervous system was telling him to fling Sven and Mr. Nubbins off his lap and run far away. But his basic family instincts wouldn't let him fling his baby cousin. His insides churned in prickly panic while his outer body froze in indecision.

Feeling Erik stiffen, Sven turned to look up. He lifted

the squirrel with both hands, as if to say, *My dear cousin, you seem ill at ease. Here is a squirrel ear to suck on. It always helps set me to rights.*

As Mr. Nubbins came closer to his to his face, Erik's panic broke free the only way it could. He screamed, "NOOOOOOOOOOOOOOOOOOOOOOOOOOOOOOOO OOIT'SGONNAEATMYFACEILIKEMYFACEDON'T LETITEATMYFACEAAAAAAAAAAAAAAAAAAA AAARRRRRRRRKLIKKAKLAKKAKLASKAKL-OPATZKLATSCHABATTACREPPYCROTTYGRA DDAGHSEMMIHSAMMIHNOUITHAPPLUDDY-APPLADDYPKONPKOTRRRRRRRRRRRRRR RRWHOOOOOOOOOOOOOAAAAAAAAAAA TAKEITAWAYTAKEITAWAYTAKEITAWAY!"

Sven leaned back, lowered Mr. Nubbins, and turned to look at Allyson for help. *Hey, he doesn't seem to want a squirrel ear right now. How do we handle this?*

Allyson started to crawl over to remove Sven from Erik's lap, but Brunhilde stopped her. "No, we have to wait until Erik exhausts himself. It may take hours. Days, even. But it is the best thing for him."

Erik kept screaming. The Dragon Breathing tech-

niques helped his volume. "PLEASEPLEASENO-
THERAPYNOWJUSTSAVEMESAVEMEOOOOOOO
OOOOOOOOOOOOOOOOOOOOOOOOOOOOOOOO
OOOOOOOOOOOOOOOOULLHODTURDENWEIR-
MUDGAARDGRINGNIRURDRMOLNIRFENRIR-
LUKKILOKKIBAUGIMANDODRRERINSURTKRIN-
MGERNRACKINAROCKAROOOOOOOOOOOOOOO
OOOOOOOOOOOOOOOOOOOOOOOOOOOOOOOO
OOOOOOOOOOOHELPHELPHELPHELPHELPITS-
EYESITSEYESITHASSUCHSCARYEYESGLAAAARR
RRRRRRRRRRRRRRRRRRRRRRRRRRRRRRRRRR
RRRRRRRRRRRRRRRK!"

Sven gazed around the circle in consternation. Seeing that the older kids weren't doing anything, the baby
boy took matters into his own tiny hands. He curled up
and slid off Erik, taking Mr. Nubbins with him. He scoot-
crawled to a corner of the room, dragging the squirrel in
his mouth by its scruff, looking over his shoulder as if
to say, *Someday you will see the value in squirrel ears,
cousin. Also, your lap is only nice when you are quiet.
Nubs and I will find somewhere else to chill.* Mr. Nubbins hung limply.

As soon as the two of them were behind a chair, Erik stopped screaming and started panting.

"Too bad." Brunhilde shrugged. "I thought you could have made some real headway there. I suppose I must plan a better way to expose you with no possibility of escape. It'll be hard to do it this week, since I am helping Aunt Hilda sand and paint the addition to the house, but I will find a way."

She had barely finished her sentence when Erik scrambled out the door and locked himself in the bathroom. Grabbing a bath towel, he wiped his face dry of sweat.

Why can't my sister leave well enough alone? he thought. *I respect my elders, but darn it, she's only six years older than me! Someday I'm going to say no and have her listen,* he thought. Inside his guts, among the post-squirrel fear splinters, he felt something new. Something solid. Something that didn't want to keep enduring whatever Brunhilde told him to do. Something that wanted to take a stand.

He rubbed his stomach. *And how do we do that?* He flicked through his mental list of Erik-style Lore and didn't see how advice about butter and salt could help him. Then he suddenly remembered that the Lake Park mountain bike team was meeting again this afternoon. *"He who can avoid stuff will not be destroyed by stuff,"* he murmured.

He rubbed his stomach again and considered. *Well . . . I could try to figure out how to take a stand, or I could find as ways to AVOID Brunhilde's exposure therapy plans as long as possible. Mountain bike practice, helping build or clean stuff, taking care of the triplets — I can keep pretty busy.*

That felt like it made sense. He went to go look for Uncle Bjorn to find out what jobs he could do that would keep him on the other side of the house from Bru.

~

After helping to organize his uncle's tools and gulping down a quick lunch, Erik got permission to walk over to the park. Allyson appeared with a shoulder bag as he was getting ready to leave. "Going to meet the mountain bikers? I'll walk you over!" she said.

It turned out Allyson's bag was full of picnic supplies. She spread a blanket out to wait for the team to appear, beaming as soon as Dylan pedaled up. Dylan owned his own mountain bike, so it was the only one not covered with sponsorship stickers. Instead it had a personalized license plate that said THE DYLAN in blue letters.

"Hi, remember me, I'm Allyson? How do you spell your name?" she asked him.

"That'd be *D-y-l-a-n*," he said.

She called out, "Give me a *D,* give me a *Y,* give me an *L-A-N!* If he can't ride it, no one can! Goooooooo, DYLAN!" The object of her affection came over to the picnic blanket to check out the tasty snacks she'd brought.

Erik left the two of them to their munching as soon as he saw Fuzz, who had carpooled with Coach Gary and two other riders. Fuzz told Erik they were going to learn things called nollies and stoppies today. Coach Gary said, "Feel free to hang back and watch until you feel comfortable joining in, Erik. No rush."

Spending the afternoon with the Lake Park All-Stars was the perfect antidote to Erik's morning squirrel madness. Coach Gary's low-key teaching style was different than anything Erik had experienced before. Erik didn't hear him once criticize anybody; instead, he focused on encouraging whatever bits went right. The coach's positive mood was contagious. The other kids spent as much time laughing and supporting each other as nollie-ing and stoppie-ing. Erik mostly practiced riding in circles, and everyone seemed fine with that.

Erik saw Brunhilde at dinner, but she seemed preoccupied with other thoughts and didn't bring up attacking his fears. And when they met for Dragon Breathing on the following mornings, she didn't say anything when Erik firmly closed the door and made sure it was latched against all babies and squirrels before settling on his pillow.

Allyson came with him to the park again on Friday for the next mountain bike practice. (After practice on Wednesday, Allyson had called her parents to ask if she could stay a couple of weeks longer with her aunt and uncle and come home the same time as Erik and Brunhilde. "I'm, like, helping and stuff?" she explained. Her mother said it was fine as long as she took on her share of triplet care.)

Allyson once again ignored Erik in favor of gazing

at Dylan, which suited Erik fine. He joined the riders in weaving back and forth between a set of six orange cones, taking it super slow, and not losing control of his bike even once.

"Errr-ik!" called Derek as he passed the final cone.

"See, he's good, right?" said Fuzz.

Erik went back to the end of the line to try it again. And again. And again.

Both Ragnar and Allyson came along on Sunday. Ragnar immediately joined a rugby scrum and was pummeling fellow players up and down the playing field in no time. When the guy who owned the rugby ball had to go home, Ragnar wandered over to watch the Lake Park All-Stars attempt a synchronized bunny hop over a ditch. (Erik practiced his own mini hop over a dandelion.) Dylan made it across the ditch. Everyone else ended up laughing in a heap in the mud.

Coach Gary laughed too. "Didn't you hear me say *bunny hop,* not *muddy flop*? Oh well, we'll get it next time. Everyone okay?" They were. The coach seemed to be wildly successful at keeping his team free from serious injuries. "A reminder, folks, that we are now two weeks away from the big race, and I've got an entry form for each of you. Please remember to fill out your bike's business sponsor's name and have your guardians sign the waiver. Bring them back to me Wednesday, and we'll start doing some training on the actual course over there." He pointed up the hill toward a thick section of woods.

Erik picked up an entry form and walked over to Allyson and Ragnar.

Ragnar said, "Can I see that?" After reading over the paper, he grinned. "Wow, cousin, that's amazing! Let's go tell the rest of the family your plan."

Erik waved goodbye to the team as they dispersed for the day. Allyson was sketching a picture of Dylan's face on her forearm and didn't want to be disturbed, so he and Ragnar started back toward the house without her.

Ragnar said, "That must be one amazing coach. In a few practices, you went from constantly hiding under things to entering the Race Down Bonebreaker Hill."

"The race down what, now?" Erik asked.

"You know, this mountain bike race," Ragnar

explained, waving the entry form. "They had to cancel it a few years back because too many kids were taken away in ambulances at the finish line. Mom wouldn't even let me do it, she said I soaked too many pairs of pants with blood and she was running out of material to sew new ones. Bonebreaker Hill is definitely a challenge fit for a Viking! How many pairs of pants do you have? Do you think it's enough? Maybe you can borrow some of my old ones. I have a maroon-colored pair, barely shows bloodstains at all."

Erik pressed his hands on either side of his forehead to keep his brain from exploding. "Are you kidding me?"

"You know a Sheepflattener never kids about blood," Ragnar said. "See? Check it out." He handed the paper over to Erik, who saw that indeed, the title of the race he had agreed to enter was THE RACE DOWN BONE-BREAKER HILL, sponsored by the Way Northern Minnesota Youth Mountain Bike Association (WNMYMBA). There was a disclaimer at the bottom stating

Participants agree that barreling down Bonebreaker Hill on two wheels is an inherently dangerous activity. No participant shall hold responsible the WNMYMBA for grievous harm or utter destruction of bicycle, clothing, or body, including loss of limbs or organs detached and reinserted into unfamiliar areas. Enjoy the ride!

Underneath was a space for the date, the rider's signature, and a guardian's signature.

Well, that's the end of that, Erik thought with more than a twinge of disappointment. *Might as well recycle this form right now, because there's no way I'm signing my name to agree to any sentences with the words* grievous harm *and* utter destruction *in them.*

When they arrived home, Ragnar immediately started bragging to the whole family about Erik's decision to enter the Race Down Bonebreaker Hill.

Aunt Hilda made a tsking sound. "Well, I'll go find some patches for your pants, Erik," she said.

"Och, Bonebreaker Hill," mused Uncle Bjorn. "A fine challenge, that place is. Hard to get through it on two feet, let alone two wheels. Did you know it was named for Bill Bonebreaker, the best dogsledder this area's ever seen? Nearby Tarantula Lake was named for his lead sled dog, Tarantula. And Man-Eating Shark River is named after his best breeding dog, Man-Eating Shark." He paused. "I never noticed before how misleading some of those names are."

Brunhilde's eyes lit up while reading the race entry paperwork. Before bedtime, she spent an hour arranging a new section made out of Legos on her three-dimensional map of Erik's fears. Erik sat watching her work, interrupting her with his protests that he could not, repeat, could NOT race down Bonebreaker Hill. She deflected his every word with an impatient grunt or a firm "Erik, yes!"

"Brunhilde, no," he whimpered. "Let's hang out and read *Garfield,* or eat popcorn instead." He looked inside himself, but the solid something in his guts that made him think he could take a stand against his sister was nowhere to be found. It was just fears and phobias all over the place in there.

Brunhilde moved a tin soldier and said, "No time for that. Brother, you cannot see how excellent this really is. We will continue our daily Dragon Breathing, you will practice mountain biking, and in two weeks, you will conquer every fear in one fell swoop." Brunhilde brought her arm down in a chopping motion. "I will explain to your coach, one campaign leader to another, how important this is. It will be glorious. Glorious. You will never be the same."

"I don't want to never be the same," Erik said. He was thinking how the race form had said something about limbs being detached and reinserted in unfamiliar areas.

Brunhilde made the chopping motion again. "Go to sleep, brother. Tomorrow I will show you how very Viking this is going to be."

Brunhilde the freight train was barreling down the track. Erik went to bed, but it was hard to fall asleep. He kept trying envision a way to say no to his sister that would sink into that rock-hard head of hers. He had to do it in a way that was very Viking, but what was that going to mean? As far as he could remember, the Lore said nothing, absolutely nothing, about coping with bossy older sisters.

TWELVE

THE QUICKSAND OF QUITTING

When tired, sleep. When hungry, eat.
When faced with the unknown, stand up
straight with your shoulders back.
— The Lore

Erik could not focus the next morning during breathing practice, thinking about how he'd tell Coach Gary and Fuzz he was quitting, not to mention how to tell Brunhilde and make it stick. It was such a shame that mountain biking had to shift so fast off the list of things he was interested in doing and onto the list of things he couldn't possibly do.

He also kept opening his eyes to look at the *ERIK VS. EVERYTHING* board spread on the coffee table next to the pillow circle. Brunhilde's new Lego construction was a long, thick hill labeled *BONEBREAKER* with a piece of masking tape. She'd put the wooden turtle at the top on a mini skateboard, and arranged little Lego animals and people each holding various weapons down the hillside. She had somehow created pits of spikes and trees with swords for leaves. She had used exclusively red bricks to build the hill itself. No other colors. *Why does she have to use so much red? Doesn't she know how much it looks like a bloody combat zone? Duh, of course she does.*

Wednesday afternoon, Brunhilde and Allyson walked Erik over to the Lake Park for the next training session. Every few steps he would think about how much he didn't want to quit, and how much he didn't want to not quit. Then he'd try to run back to his aunt and uncle's house, but one of his sisters would snag him by a belt loop.

Allyson said, "You have to stay part of this team, Erik.

Anything that Dylan is a part of is super cool. I'll keep coming to every practice with you, plus I can help you decide what to wear. Doesn't that make you feel totes fab-yoo-lous?"

"Do you not see?" Brunhilde exhorted him. "This way we need not set up any complicated situations to expose you to exposure therapy. The Race Down Bonebreaker Hill will do it for us. Let us count. There will be" — she started ticking things off on her fingers — "potential for embarrassment, plus criticism with the spectators watching the race, a nice big opportunity to fail since you have had little training, and lots of chances to experience pain and get bloody. I assume those woods are full of wild animals, too. I have heard silent and speedy bike riders can accidentally sneak up on forest animals and then the animals attack in a frenzy. Mr. Nubbins will have nothing on a startled wild mama squirrel. Or a raccoon. Or maybe a badger! Make no mistake, this is your battleground."

They were the first people there. Coach Gary was setting up orange cones in a big circle.

"Erik, my Hair Shack Hero!" he said. He raised his hand for a high-five. "Don't leave me hanging, dude-a-roni."

Erik weakly slapped Gary's hand. "Hi, Coach. I, uh, I'm sorry, but I need to talk to you about the race."

Brunhilde broke in. "This is the most wonderful opportunity for my brother. Riding in this race means more to him than you can know. Hurtling downhill into danger is so very Viking. What species of carnivorous animals live on Bonebreaker Hill? Exactly how many broken bones per rider do you expect?"

Coach Gary opened his hands. "I know, I know, the race has had a really bad reputation. But things have changed. The organizers this year have done a lot of work to make it much safer. The race route no longer includes Deadman's Cliff or the Quicksand Swamp. By the way, did you know the swamp was named after dogsledder Bill Bonebreaker's wife, Quinn "Quicksand" Bonebreaker? Anyway, I guarantee you our team is focused one hundred percent on having fun and staying safe and sound. We're here to learn some bike-handling skills, support each other, and have a great time. If someone wins a ham, so much the better. As long as we get through race day without getting hurt."

Brunhilde frowned. "How unexpected." She thought for a minute. "I think I understand. If your troops concentrate on bike-handling skills and working together, they will not focus too much on the hazards and dangers. They will give the impression that all they care about is fun." She turned to Erik. "Sun Tzu also recommends this tactic: *Offer the enemy a bait to lure him; feign disorder and strike him. Pretend inferiority and encourage his arrogance.* If you pretend to train for fun, your phobias will become weak and lazy, unprepared. Then when you expose yourself to the fears during the race, you will be stronger than they are." She gave a pleased grunt.

Erik looked at Allyson to see if she was following whatever Brunhilde was talking about. Allyson wasn't paying any attention now that Dylan had ridden up. He smiled at Allyson and treated her to his chin-jutting "'sup" greeting. Allyson clasped her hands together and sighed.

"Oh, Fricka's socks, what is happening to her?" Brunhilde muttered. "It seems I cannot leave Allyson alone here." She asked Coach Gary, "Would you like another volunteer to help you prepare for the race? I know little of bicycle skills, but I know much of training a force to overcome obstacles. Have you read Sun Tzu?"

"*The Art of War*? As a matter of fact, I have. We're studying it in my college marketing class," Coach Gary said. "You think Sun Tzu could apply to mountain biking?" The two of them began talking about harnessing war tactics to improve cycling, and Erik wandered over to where Fuzz was exiting his mom's car.

"Hi, Fuzz," he said.

"Erik, hey!" Fuzz responded. "Looks like we're going to do interval endurance drills today, those are tricky. Gotta push hard enough to finish but not so hard you hurl your lunch."

"I don't think I'm going to be doing them," Erik said. He cleared his throat. "I'm telling Coach Gary today I can't be on the team anymore."

Fuzz looked crushed. "Oh man, that stinks! For some reason, it's really hard to get kids to join up. I think it's because everyone has heard that the race is so dangerous."

"Isn't it?" asked Erik. "I mean, aren't you worried about it?"

"Worried? Nah," Fuzz responded. "Coach Gary's so serious about getting us through the season without any major injuries. I think I've learned better how to fall down than how to ride, to be honest." As he talked, he tripped over a rock and grabbed Erik's shoulder to steady himself. "See? My mom says I was born accident-prone. I think she signed me up for this so I could learn how to avoid getting hurt so much. I mean, I got more scrapes and bruises from doing a sew-your-own-stuffed-animal class than I have being out here with the team." Fuzz looked at Erik. "Can't you stay? It's less than two weeks until the race. And you're getting really good."

Erik thought about it. He wasn't getting really good. But no one seemed to care about that. Fuzz genuinely liked having him here, and he liked hanging out with Fuzz. He wished there were a way to get out of racing Bonebreaker Hill without having to quit or take a stand against anyone. He asked, "Do I have to do the race? Could I keep coming to practice and then skip the race?"

"Maybe," Fuzz said. "Let's ask Coach Gary. Would you stay if you didn't have to do the race? Say yes, say yes!" Fuzz stumbled over his own shoelaces. "I'll even give you my free packet of seeds from the garden center."

"Thanks, I guess, but I don't know if this will work," Erik said.

Fuzz and Erik joined Brunhilde and Coach Gary. Brunhilde told the boys, "Good news. I am going to help with your practice sessions to prepare for the race by explaining Sun Tzu's theories on waging a successful war. Your team will be unstoppable."

Oh, man. Erik tried to envision how Coach Gary's cheerful let's-all-have-fun-out-there attitude would combine with his sister's take-no-prisoners outlook, and it made him dizzy. He looked miserably at Fuzz.

"Coach Gary," Fuzz said, "Erik is not a racing kind of kid. He's a practicing kind of kid. Can he just keep practicing with the team and watch the race instead? Is that okay?"

Erik tried to summon some of the solid feeling in his guts and added, "I don't mind doing bunny hops and muddy flops, but bone breaking is way more than I can handle."

Other riders gathered as the discussion progressed.

"Don't give up, Erik, we need a Hair Shack Hero," said Lily. The others joined in.

"Yeah, you just mastered the drop! You are doing so good!"

"Keep training with us."

"'Sup. Are you new?"

"We gotta keep the team together! All for one and one for all!"

"Aren't you having fun?"

Coach Gary was unfazed. He said, "How about this: keep training, bring me the paperwork next time, and wait and see how you feel about race day on race day. You might surprise yourself."

"Yes," said Brunhilde. "Why not wait and see?"

Erik liked Coach Gary's wait-and-see encouragement face more than his sister's wait-and-see-because-this-is-going-to-happen-and-you-cannot-escape face. He also liked the faces of his teammates looking expectantly back at him. Every other time he'd quit an activity, everyone seemed relieved to see him go. This time, they actually wanted him to stick around. Then again, they'd only seen Erik the Decent Mountain Biker Kid Who Can Fall Down Pretty Well. They'd never seen him facing a fear. He wanted to keep it that way.

He rubbed the back of his neck. If he kept practicing, maybe he could use the days leading up to the competition to find a way to say no to his sister that would stick. Brunhilde was planning to help the team learn war strategies using Sun Tzu or whatever? Well, he'd turn the tables on her. He bet if he listened closely to the strategy stuff she kept spouting, he'd find some wisdom about fighting off a sister. And then he'd throw it back in her face. And then probably run away fast.

"Okay, okay, fine," he said. "I guess I'll wait and see." *I'll wait and see how I'm going to AVOID this race.*

"Hooray, Hair Shack Hero is in the house!" yelled Fuzz.

"Whoop whoop," one of the other riders sang out, and

a group of them started doing a hip-swinging dance together.

"Are we going to start practicing now?" asked Dylan, stretching his arms over his head. "We gotta be in it to win it, yo." Allyson scampered over to his side and offered to rub his shoulders.

Before she could reach the boy's shoulders, Brunhilde lunged over to grab both of Allyson's hands and announced, "We've got to go do some things at home now, sister of mine." She pulled Allyson away from Dylan and gave Dylan the same kind of you'd-better-watch-yourself look the triplets gave strangers who tried to tickle them.

She steered Allyson toward the path home and said over her shoulder to Erik, "We'll be back on Friday to help plan your assault on the hill."

THIRTEEN

BONEBREAKER HILL

Fight downhill.

–Sun Tzu, *The Art of War*

The next practice began at the trailhead leading into the thick pine forest. Coach Gary said, "Gather round, gang. Today we start to train on the actual course for the Race Down Bonebreaker Hill," to the assembled Lake Park All-Stars. "We're going to walk it first and see where some of the more difficult sections come up. I'll also point out the dangerous portions of the trail that are off-limits. And I want to introduce everyone to Erik's sister Brunhilde. She offered to help us map the trail and come up with our best tactics for each part of the course."

"Greetings, All-Stars," Brunhilde said gravely. "I believe that what Coach Gary is saying can be summed up by the ancient Chinese general Sun Tzu: *Know the enemy and know yourself; in a hundred battles you will never be in peril.*" She had her purple notebook turned to a fresh page that she had labeled *MOUNTAIN BIKERS VS. BONEBREAKER HILL.*

"I think what Brunhilde is saying is if we learn the course, we can rock the course," said Gary as he swung a backpack over his shoulder.

"I think what Coach Gary is saying is we will throw rocks at you if you cannot learn this course," said Brunhilde.

"Is that what you thought I was saying?" asked Gary.

"Is that not what you were saying?" asked Brunhilde.

They looked at each other. Coach Gary shook his head like he was waking up from a confusing dream. "Anyway, let's go check out Bonebreaker Hill, gang!"

The team left their bikes stacked together against a tall fir tree. Coach Gary led the way into the shade.

Allyson was with the group, carrying a sack lunch she had packed for Dylan. Although it was a sunny summer day, inside the old-growth forest it was ten degrees cooler and a little gloomy. A rabbit darted under a bush, fluffy white tail flashing, and two bored-looking crows watched them from a branch. Erik felt a small pang of anxiety, but walking surrounded by his teammates was honestly not that scary. He'd take hanging out here over riding a school bus any day of the week.

Coach Gary said, "Each group will take off at timed intervals by age here. We'll start on this nice, wide fire road, but then you'll soon see the racecourse heads out on some twisty singletrack." He indicated a skinny trail further downhill. "So try to pick up some speed on the fire road when you can."

Brunhilde sketched the first part of the map and said, *"Speed is the essence of war."*

They continued on, feet sliding on the pine needles covering the slope.

"You'll be fine on the roller-coaster-ish course section here. Gravity will do a lot of work for you. Watch out for these couple of rock-choked chutes." Coach Gary showed them some areas with rocks the size of fists. "Coming up next, we have the deadfall. Every winter, trees get knocked down by giant snows, so this area always has logs and branches every which way. You can find the trail by following the red ribbons tied around posts over there," Coach Gary pointed them out. "This is going to take some hopping and dropping, but remember if you feel like the hop is beyond you, dismount and walk it. Slow and steady wins the race, and . . . ?"

"Let's keep our teeth in our face," recited the team in unison, except for Dylan who said, "All that matters is first place." Everyone else ignored him.

The group came to a sunny spot where there was a break in the trees. Enormous boulders sat like sentries. Cliffs with dark openings yawned down at them from overhead.

Coach Gary continued, "Watch here for any rocks looking to munch your tires. And up there are the bear caves," he explained. "Just to be on the safe side, we're equipping every rider with bear bells." He took a set out of his backpack and jingled them. "Nothing good can happen when you startle a bear while on a bike, so we'll make sure you broadcast your arrival with the bells and they'll get out of your way before you ever get near them."

Erik looked up at the caves and shivered. The bear bells didn't sound anywhere near menacing enough to drive bears out of the cyclists' way. In fact, they sounded kind of festive and inviting, like old-time dinner bells. *Come and get it, hungry bears! Thanksgiving dinner has arrived early!* He noticed some thick wads of sticks in the tallest tree branches and raised his hand. "What are those things up there?" he asked.

"Raptor nests. Goshawks and owls mostly, I understand. Do you notice there aren't any chipmunks or squirrels hopping around here? The birds of prey have decimated their populations in this area," Coach Gary said.

"Oh." Erik cautiously thought he might be happy about that, although he wasn't sure how he felt about birds of prey. He decided it was best not to think too hard about the whole situation.

"Now, Brunhilde, please make sure this is clear on the map." Coach Gary walked over to a side path where someone had laid down a large fallen tree trunk and spray-painted a black X. Coach Gary took a yellow spool of caution tape out of his backpack and ran a loop of tape around the trunk. "I'm going to mark this again for good measure. This used to be the path that led riders over Deadman's Cliff and into the swamp. We don't use this route anymore, so whatever you do, DON'T take this side track. It's crazy back there. Not even fit for adult master's-level riders."

Brunhilde carefully labeled this section of her map with a skull and crossbones. She said, "I believe Coach Gary is calling upon this bit of Sun Tzu's wisdom: *There are some roads not to follow; some troops not to strike; some cities not to assault; and some ground which should not be contested.*"

Erik's ears perked up. This was the first time he'd heard Brunhilde quote anything about not fighting. This sounded like advice about AVOIDING STUFF. He made a mental note, and wondered if Sun Tzu had any older sisters.

Coach Gary said, "I believe Brunhilde is saying that part of the hill is not any fun on two wheels."

"And I believe I am saying you should annihilate the rest of the hill on two wheels. And pulverize any fears you find along the way. That will be fun," Brunhilde added.

"I believe Brunhilde is saying . . ." Gary trailed off, then shook his head again like he was waking up from another dream. "Right! Okay, after the deadfall, there's the wet section." They were now slogging through some muddy areas where tiny streams crossed the course. "See how there are some plank bridges? It'll be up to each of you to decide if you want to try the bridge or go straight through the water. It's slippery either way, so again, you'll need to focus. Further down we get to the Holey Meadow, where you need to keep your eyes out for the trail markers so you don't end up lodging your wheel in a sinkhole or mole hole or fox hole. And from there we're back to singletrack."

Here they were walking on a trail etched on the hill in the shape of a zigzag with sharp turns to the left and right. "These are the switchbacks. Tricky, but at the end, our old friend gravity will be waiting to help you across the finish line. Did I mention before there will be cookies at the finish line? How could I forget to mention the cookies? Most important part. So, any questions?"

Lily raised her hand. "Can my mom and dad come watch the race?" she asked.

"Oh yeah, families are so welcome to come!" Coach Gary answered. "There's plenty of room at the start and finish for crowds of fans, and they'll have some vans shuttling people around from the top to the bottom so your family can cheer for you on both ends. They just don't let spectators on the course itself. Not after the Unexpected Mosquito Swarm of '08."

Erik asked timidly, "Was that named after Bill Bonebreaker's tiny, harmless kitten Mosquito?"

"Nope, it was named after a surprising swarm of mosquitoes nearly as big as your hand taking over the area. I hear it was like being chased by vampires. But I'm sure that won't happen again," Coach Gary reassured him.

Erik waited to see if Brunhilde had anything to add from Sun Tzu, but she seemed fine with the possibility of vampire mosquitoes. She continued sketching in her notebook during the whole walk back up the hill. When it was time to wrap things up for the day, she said, "On Sunday, I will bring copies of the map so you may study it yourselves at home. Preparation is key."

Coach Gary began, "I believe Brunhilde is saying . . ."

Brunhilde looked at him impassively.

"That preparation is key," Coach Gary finished. "So let's line up by age, oldest first, and try out this first section together. Remember, power of positive visualization: if you think you can clear that rock, you can. Look ahead to what's coming up. It's not the destination, it's the journey. Saddle up!"

The Lake Park All-Stars gamely took on the first part of the racecourse as a group, younger kids like Lily, Erik, and Fuzz behind the older riders, with Coach Gary bringing up the rear and shouting advice. The short practice session was more fun than the drills they'd been doing in the park. Everyone was focused on their own bikes, so Erik didn't feel self-conscious about pitting himself against roots and rocks. He forgot about the bear caves and raptor nests and mosquito swarms and lost himself in slow-motion balancing, bunny hops, and boulders.

Sunday, Brunhilde brought copies of her *MOUNTAIN BIKERS VS. BONEBREAKER HILL* map for everyone. Fuzz unrolled his copy and whistled. He said, "This looks like something out of *The Hobbit*."

So it did. Erik had to admit the map was a thing of beauty. Brunhilde taken it upon herself to name the sections of the course and add inspirational quotes from Sun Tzu and Viking mythology. She had even sketched animals and trees in the margins, including a hungry-looking family of bears. In the off-limits portion that led to Deadman's Cliff, she'd put a gaping mouth full of fangs and the legend *Here There Be Dragons*.

Brunhilde had labeled the eight portions of the course thus:

- *THE ROAD OF FIRE*
- *ROLLERCOASTER ROCK CHUTE*
- *DEADFALL OF DOOM*
- *BEARS TAKE THE HINDMOST*
- *SLIPPERY SLASH*
- *HOLEY MEADOW*

- *SLICE AND DICE*
- *THE FINISH (WITH COOKIES FOR THE PRAISEWORTHY)*

She had also made a special copy for Erik on which she had overlaid his phobias in red pencil, showing *EMBARRASSMENT* and *CRITICISM* at the start and finish lines with very realistic representations of Mrs. Loathcraft and his fourth-grade teacher, Mr. Sullivan, holding both battle-axes and telephones, *PAIN* and *BLOOD* in the Deadfall of Doom section, *FAILURE* represented by flat bike tires through pretty much every section of the course, and *SQUIRRELS* in the thickly forested areas, represented by an eerily cute, smiling creature that was somehow much scarier than the bears or dragons.

Erik pinched his copy of the map between his fingertips and didn't bother to study it. He'd come up with an alternate strategy for race day after pondering Brunhilde's Art of War advice: *Know the enemy and know yourself; in a hundred battles you will never be in peril.* He knew Brunhilde well enough to know arguing with her was pointless. He knew himself well enough to know that he was really good at hiding under stuff. So he'd determined that his best bet would be to locate a fool-proof hiding spot inside Uncle Bjorn and Aunt Hilda's house, pack up some jerky and water the night before the race, and then hide until it was time to go back to Connecticut. It wasn't the most exciting plan, but it played to his strengths.

"Lake Park All-Stars, lend me your ears." Brunhilde's voice rang out and echoed through the entire park. The riders gazed at her. She held the map over her head. "We shall not flag or fail. We shall go on to the end. We shall fight in the forest, we shall fight in the mud and on the boulders, we shall fight on the singletrack, whatever the cost may be. We shall fight on the rock chutes, we shall fight on the meadows, we shall fight in the hills and through the tricky bits with the fallen branches. We shall NEVER SURRENDER!"

Surrender ... surrender ... surrender continued echoing for a half minute after she was done.

All the mountain bikers stared at her, mouths agape (except Dylan, who was cleaning his fingernails with a tire lever and appeared to have missed the whole speech).

"Right," Brunhilde continued, "everyone look at the start of your maps, beginning with the Road of Fire." She began describing the course to them in terms of battle tactics. The riders closed their gaping mouths and got down to work, asking questions to clarify what she meant by "attack from above" and "never relinquish the high ground."

Coach Gary came closer to Erik and looked over his shoulder at the personalized phobia map. Coach Gary traced the picture Brunhilde had drawn of Mrs. Loath-craft with a pickaxe at the finish line. "Brunhilde sure has some imagination!"

"You have no idea," Erik said.

"So, do I understand right that you are pretty scared about race day?" Coach Gary asked.

Erik nodded.

"The first time most people try anything, it can feel pretty scary. But I'm hoping you can overcome your nerves for your pal Fuzz. I was talking to Fuzz's mom, and she's pretty worried about him riding the course without a friend to keep an eye on him every inch of the way. I told her we had another cautious, stable rider we could count on to be Fuzz's race day buddy—you. You really seem to have a handle on the safety techniques I've been teaching."

Erik squirmed uncomfortably under Coach Gary's friendly gaze. He snuck a glance at his map and saw the knowing smirk of the red-pencil squirrel.

"I don't know, Coach Gary . . ." he started.

"Hear me out. Once you and Fuzz cross the start line, if things feel too hairy, you can both walk your bikes along the entire course. One of you may even end up being the *lanterne rouge*. That's the 'red lantern' in French. It's what they call the last guy to cross the Tour de France finish line each day, the guy who hung on and didn't give up or get disqualified. Can you at least try to do that for me? For Fuzz?" He smiled hopefully. "Our Hair Shack Hero? Remember, you get a free trim after race day. And there will be cookies."

Erik looked at his teammates listening to Brunhilde explain the finer points of waging war. Fuzz was bouncing up and down and saying, "I think I get it, I think I get it! It's like when Coach Gary says you have to ride your bike instead of letting it ride you!" Brunhilde shook her head patiently and started again from the top.

"I'll try," Erik answered, looking at his shoes. He didn't mean it. He wanted Coach Gary to stop talking to him in such a nice and reasonable way.

Coach Gary beamed as if Erik had agreed whole-heartedly instead of feebly withdrawing from their conversation. "I'll take it," Coach Gary said. "I know you won't let us down." He went over to lead the group down to Rollercoaster Rock Chute and start the day's practice drills.

How could you possibly know that? Erik thought. His stomach swayed. Now how was he going to keep himself safe from the race, safe from Brunhilde, and safe from failing Fuzz and his coach? There wasn't a bed big enough in all of Minnesota to hide him from this. He needed advice on how to create an antibattle battle plan of his own, and he simply wasn't good enough at inventing Erik-style Lore yet. His eye fell on the slim red cover of *The Art of War* in Brunhilde's hand. There had to be more useful stuff in there. He decided he'd try reading it right away see if Sun Tzu had any more to say about how some roads were not to be followed—maybe there were ancient tactics for detouring around battles entirely.

Fuzz called his name, waving him over to join the group. "Thanks for saying you'd ride with me during the race!" Fuzz said, beaming. Even his hair looked happy, boinging out of the vents in his helmet.

"About that—" Erik started to say, but Fuzz kept talking.

"My mom wasn't going to let me try, but knowing I'll have a riding buddy made her agree I could give it a shot. C'mon, let's catch up with everyone."

Erik pedaled after him. There was nothing to he could do for now but roll down a rock-riddled trail.

FOURTEEN

THE ART OF WAR

As long as there is breath in your body, plus
half a minute more, fight on, fight on, fight on.
— The Lore

Erik went looking through Brunhilde's stuff at home, but couldn't find where she'd put *The Art of War* book. He went looking again the next morning after Dragon Breathing, but still had no luck.

Hrolf found him wiggling back out from checking under Brunhilde's bed. He informed Erik that the triplets had had an especially sticky and smelly breakfast, so the two boys had been given the duty of airing them out before naptime. They pushed the stroller into town.

"Let's stop in the library. I think we need more nap-time stories for Sven," Hrolf suggested. Sven did love listening to Fanny Fearless stories before naps, even more than the epic Sheepflattener war poems. They made their way to the children's department, and Erik helped Hrolf sift through the new board books, looking for Fanny's trademark orange cover.

"Look!" Hrolf held up a book with a sleeping walrus on the front. "*The Art of Snore*! That's like Brunhilde's war book, isn't it?" He opened the first page and read aloud to Sven. "*We have had our time to roar / We have had our time to soar / So we lie upon the floor / And practice now the Art of Snore.* What do you think?"

Sven made a yucky face.

"Yeah, that's nowhere near as good as *Fanny Fearless Frees a Finch*." Hrolf tossed it in the reject pile.

Erik checked out the snore book's back cover. It said THE NEWEST CLASSIC FROM THE BEST-SELLING AUTHOR OF THE TODDLER ART OF WAR!

There's a toddler version of The Art of War? Erik looked in the board book cubby labeled with the letter *T* and pulled out a book entitled *The Toddler Art of War*.

It was about the same size as Brunhilde's copy of *The Art of War* with a picture on the cover of two toddlers facing off in a preschool classroom. Each held one leg of a stuffed elephant, and neither looked ready to let go. There was a quote on the front from some businessman saying, "In our competitive world, your children need every advantage. If you expect your preschoolers to be winners, you must read them *The Toddler Art of War*."

Erik flipped through it. Written next to drawings of animals and alphabet blocks were all the sayings from the original *Art of War*. The board book author didn't appear to have done anything to simplify them for toddlers. Erik recognized the quote Brunhilde had recited at Deadman's Cliff: *There are some roads not to follow, some troops not to strike; some cities not to assault; and some ground which should not be contested.* This was accompanied by a drawing of a fence with a mean-looking dog chained up behind it. This was a bestseller? It sure was hard to understand sometimes what books grownups bought for their kids.

"Found one!" Hrolf proudly waved *Fanny Fearless Faces a Flood*.

Erik gave him *The Toddler Art of War* and said, "Take this one out for me, too, cousin." So what if it was meant for preschoolers? If it gave him the words to take a successful stand against Brunhilde, he'd consider it the best book he'd ever read.

Erik studied the toddlers in the book and tried to come up with an escape plan that afternoon, but most of Sun Tzu's advice didn't make much sense to him, even with the colorful drawings. He still couldn't make up his mind about what to do. Every plan that began with skipping the race got short-circuited by uncomfortable visions of a massively disappointed Fuzz being dragged away from the starting line by his mom because his riding buddy was a no-show. Every plan that involved showing up at the race got short-circuited by images from Brunhilde's race map, especially that disturbingly cute squirrel at the center, smiling, smiling, smiling away.

~

Coach Gary had contacted everyone's families to ask if they could make it to two extra practices this week to prepare for the race, so Erik came to practice the very next afternoon. Coach Gary told them that more than twenty teams from around Minnesota were coming to the competition. The Lake Park All-Stars had to make the most of their sole advantage: access to the racecourse before race day.

The team drilled each section of the race thoroughly. Coach Gary had them chanting different tactics to cement them in their brains so they'd become second nature, like "Loose Wrists, No Fists" to keep their hands light on the handlebars in the Slice and Dice section. Allyson helped make up rhymes when she could, like "We don't wanna BONK, we don't wanna BIFF, so make sure your knees are not too STIFF! Gooooo, Dylan!!!"

Brunhilde added her own chants to the mix, although only Lily, the youngest rider, embraced them. The elfin eight-year-old dodged rocks and boulders, gaily singing, "The strike of a hawk breaks the body of its prey, we time our strikes in the same fearsome way!" to the tune of "Twinkle, Twinkle, Little Star."

Brunhilde had also demonstrated Dragon Breathing to the mountain bike team. Almost every rider on the team got into it, even Dylan, who muttered to himself,

"I breathe in, and I am the Dylan. I breathe out, and I am still the Dylan." Then he would smile. Erik caught himself smiling too.

Two days before the race, Coach Gary showed up with a large cardboard box. "Swag for my All-Stars!" he yelled. "Gather round!" The kids made a circle as he cut open the tape holding the box shut. "Thanks to Patsy's Print Shop"—this was the sponsor for Lily's bicycle, which had decals of the entire alphabet printed in different fonts covering the frame—"we've now got team uniforms to wear on race day. Check them out, they are too cool." He pulled open the box flaps and held up the neon yellow shirts with the name LAKE PARK ALL-STARS (EVERYONE WELCOME) emblazoned across the front and back. Every sponsor had a small logo either on the body or arms of the jersey, including the Hair Shack, Whiskers and Wings, Ed's Live Bait and Tanning Salon, the US Post Office, the Pie Slab, Hardware 'n' Stuff 'n' More, Wet Your Plants, Good Food Emporium, and Patsy's Print Shop.

Coach Gary enlisted Fuzz's help to distribute the shirts, and everyone started trying them on. Allyson cheered, "Victory, victory, victory is OURS. We're gonna win 'cause we are the STARS!" She did a toe-touch jump.

Erik admired how good the team looked in their bright uniforms. Then his inner voice piped up, *At least they'll find my body easily if the bears attack.* He shook his head hard. *No bear attacks! I'm not riding this race! I am Erik Sheepflattener, son of Inge and Thorfast, grandson of Golveg and Vigdis, brother to Brunhilde and Allyson, and I'm going to AVOID STUFF. I will have this figured out by tomorrow night.*

~

The night before the Race Down Bonebreaker Hill, Brunhilde and Allyson started a tag-team wrestling match against Ragnar and Hrolf.

Hrolf complained, "Unfair, unfair! Girls are too strong to form one team together, we're never gonna win!"

Ragnar hollered back, "Even when faced with rough, tough girls, we must never give up, brother!" He launched himself toward Allyson, crushing (or possibly smashing?) a small table in the process.

Slipping away from the chaos, Erik passed

Brunhilde's purple notebook and glittery pen unattended on the couch. He spontaneously grabbed them and hid them behind his back as he slunk down the hall. Maybe her notebook would have a blank page where he could organize his thoughts.

He closed the boys' bedroom door and lay on his back, head propped up on a pillow. Worrying plus mountain biking had worn him out. He wanted to close his eyes, but he didn't have time to be tired. *I have to have a perfect plan. Come on, brain, let's make a perfect plan.*

Before picking up *The Toddler Art of War*, he flipped through the purple notebook. He pawed through page after page of maps and lists and plans labeled in Brunhilde's careful printing: *ALLIES VS. AXIS, SPARTA VS. GREECE, MONGOL HORDE VS. THE WORLD, MINUTEMEN VS. THE REDCOATS, BRUNHILDE VS. ALGEBRA, ERIK VS. FEAR, CRUSHING VS. SMASHING*, and finally *MOUNTAIN BIKERS VS. BONEBREAKER HILL*. He flipped past a sketch without a *VS.* on it and then flipped back.

The header on this page said *ERIK + SHEEPFLATTENERS*. Brunhilde had drawn a group of people seated around a campfire with their eyes closed. He recognized Brunhilde's drawing of herself as a Valkyrie warrior, and also recognized Allyson with her cheer outfit on, Ragnar with a pike impaled on an arrow, and Hrolf holding the triplets on his lap. She had also drawn some of the grownups in the family—Aunt Hilda, Uncle Bjorn, Mom, and Dad. There were a few unfamiliar figures that might have been some of the old gods. Erik saw a sketch of himself, small and unimpressive, sandwiched between his two sisters. He noticed that Brunhilde had drawn everyone in the picture holding hands.

I wonder what this is supposed to show? he thought. *How Brunhilde's going to have everyone in my family drag me toward my fears?* Then he saw tiny printing at the bottom of the page. There were two runes. The first was FAMILY. Below it was a twisty slashing symbol that looked a lot like Brunhilde's CONQUER. Erik traced his finger over it and tried to remember the translation. "Vanquish"? No. "Pulverize"? No. Oh yes, he remembered the word now. The rune said UNCONQUERABLE. He traced the pattern over and over, and thought and thought, and yawned, and thought. Then he took out the book of warring toddlers and got to work.

~

Erik was jolted out of a doze by the sound of a knock. "No, no, don't make me share the alphabet blocks, no, no," he muttered, and then saw he was safe in bed, no toddlers anywhere. He must have fallen asleep. Ragnar and Hrolf were already in their own bunk beds nearby, snoring like dragons gargling pieces of meat.

Aunt Hilda pushed the door open. "I saw the light was still on, nephew." She came over to the trundle bed and knelt down, pulling the covers up to Erik's chin. "Big day tomorrow. You'll need your rest, so no more reading." She gathered up the board book, purple notebook, and glitter pen and set them on the floor, glancing at the open notebook page. "Or no more writing, I guess I should say." The open page had the rune for UNCONQUERABLE in Erik's slightly messy handwriting at the top. Underneath, the page had been filled from top to bottom with nothing but the words *NO* and *AVOID* surrounded by glittery question marks.

Hilda smiled. "Unconquerable. That's probably the second most tattooed rune that Sheepflatteners have chosen since the Lore was created. There's only one that's been chosen more, of course, and that's . . ." She looked down and saw Erik's eyes had drooped closed and his mouth had drooped open. He was asleep again.

She brushed the hair off his forehead and whispered, "Family." Aunt Hilda turned out the light.

FIFTEEN

RACE DAY

Never give in. Never give in,
never, never, never, never.
—The Lore (incidentally later said
by Winston Churchill, 1941)

Erik woke up with the feeling someone was watching him. He turned over and saw three pairs of eyes
peeking around the edge of his door. As soon as the
triplets were sure he was awake, they started howling
like wolf cubs. Siegmund nudged the door open with his
face, and they tumbled in, wiggle-crawling and rolling
toward the bed, drooling proudly.

"Good job, kids!" Allyson strode into his room with

a big plate of bacon, eggs, smoked salmon, toast, and dried apples. "I knew he'd wake up soon. Thanks for giving me the secret signal." She plopped the plate and a fork on Erik's lap as he pushed himself into a seated position. "Eat up, little brother. Today is your race day, and I know you'll need plenty of strength to keep up with Dylan!" She sat on the edge of the bed. "Where's your uniform? I'm going to plan my outfit to match."

Erik pointed the fork toward his All-Stars jersey, draped over the back of a chair. There was a commotion in the front hallway, and he heard his mother's loud voice. "Hilda, so wonderful to see you! Thank you for inviting us to come."

Erik froze with a forkful of eggs halfway to his mouth. "Is that *Mom?*" he asked his sister.

"Yeah! Mom and Dad came to be here for the race today. I called them to plan their visit as soon as you signed that entry form. No surprise there, right?" Allyson answered.

"Uh, big surprise there, actually. Why would you invite them to see the race?" asked Erik. *Brunhilde can now make my family drag me across that starting line.*

That is why it was so hard to come up with an escape plan. Because there is no escape. He slapped his forehead. *Stop thinking that way! You came up with a plan last night. It's going to work. It has to work.*

Allyson laughed and whacked him on the shoulder hard enough to make his stack of toast wobble. "I invited them to meet Dylan, of course. I mean, I've told Mom about him." She gazed off into space in rapture, probably imagining what she and her beloved Dylan would be wearing when they got married. She added offhandedly, "Oh, and because I am totes proud of you, Erik. This is a big deal! It's your first race, your first, like, anything, that you're going to finish all the way to the end."

Brunhilde entered the room and added, "Plus, it does not hurt to enlist a few more warriors to support you on this day. Our preparations come to this. Today your fears will know what it means to do real battle with a Sheepflattener. Your phobias will be obliterated by the time the sun sets on Bonebreaker Hill."

"Where's my boy and girls?" They heard their mother coming down the hall. "The house has been so quiet without you all!" She entered the room. "Oh, my darling beasts! Have you been good guests?" She gave Brunhilde and Allyson a hug apiece and then sat down next to Erik and ruffled his hair. "Just waking up, are we? Well, growing boys need their sleep. And you have grown. Look at you! Practically ready to build a house of your own."

Erik's father came into the room too and sat on the other side of the bed. He reached over and took a slice of bacon from Erik's plate and nodded to Erik. His mother slapped the bacon out of his father's hand. "Don't you dare, Thorfast. The boy needs all the strength he can get! Remember what Brunhilde told us about his race today."

Thorfast grabbed another slice, dodged his wife's hand, and popped the bacon in his mouth. He smiled at Erik and chewed.

"Well, let's give him time to eat and get dressed," his mom said, standing up. "You girls show me your rooms, and let's talk about what you've been up to out here in Minnesota. Did I tell you already that Spjut misses you? He sniffs under Erik's bed every day to see if he's secretly been hiding under there all summer . . ." She strolled out the door with Brunhilde and Allyson. Thorfast followed behind after palming another bacon slice.

Erik looked out the window as he got changed. He scanned the sky for clouds, wondering what the chances were that Thor would reach down from the heavens and lightning-bolt the whole racecourse into nonexistence. Figuring it couldn't hurt, he sent up a respectful appeal for all available lightning, thunder, hail, sleet, and rain to hit Bonebreaker Hill before the starting gun went off.

Family members kept wandering in and out of his room to see if he needed anything (Aunt Hilda and Allyson) or to remind him how important the day was (Brunhilde, and his mother, who wanted to check he had put on clean underwear) or to swipe food from his breakfast plate (Ragnar, Hrolf, and his father). Eventually, the food disappeared and he was dressed in his shirt, shorts, and sneakers (yes, with clean underwear). The whole family swept out the door toward the park before he had even the slightest chance to consider hiding under any beds. Good thing his new plan didn't involve them.

After working out his options, his new plan ended up being simple. First, he would cross the starting line with Fuzz and ride until they were both out of sight of Fuzz's mom. Once behind the cover of some trees, he would pretend to fall off his bike, fake a horrible upset stomach, and insist that Fuzz go on without him. Once Fuzz continued on, Erik would lie there like a hopeless slug until a race official collected him.

He knew lying limp and sluggy wouldn't necessarily save him from Brunhilde. In case she somehow intuited his giving up and stomped down the course to tie him to his bike and shove him down Bonebreaker Hill, the final piece of his plan was a whole *Art of War*–inspired speech he'd worked out. He was going to lead with "There are some roads not to follow" and then segue into "Those skilled in war subdue the enemy's army without battle" (in *The Toddler Art of War,* this advice had a picture of a kid drinking another kid's juice box behind his back). There were a few more quotes he'd memorized after that. He didn't completely understand some of them, but he was sure he would be telling her NO in warrior language. In fact, he was going end by telling her that saying NO was very Viking. Then he would go the limpest and slug-giest he'd ever gone and, copying his sister's stubborn-ness, refuse to listen to anything else anyone had to say. Maybe he couldn't hide, but he surely could do nothing.

He didn't give up hope that Thor might demolish the course, though. If he'd learned one thing from listening to his family's old epic poems, it was that lightning bolts could and did strike when they were least expected.

~

Lake Park had been transformed into a hive of mountain bikers. Twenty teams of nine riders had registered, and each one was clustered together wearing matching jerseys. A registration table was set up where riders got their numbers and their guardians signed the "grievous harm" waiver if they hadn't already done so. Officials dressed in black with the word RACE STAFF stitched in white on their backs were making sure all was in order. A big black screen showed a digital clock that would track the length of the race with red numbers glowing 00:00:00 to show hours, minutes, and seconds. A fleet of passenger vans were ready to bring spectators down to the finish line once all the riders were on the course. Local newspaper writers and television reporters were there to cover the story of the big Race Down Bonebreaker Hill.

One television reporter with unusually white teeth

addressed a video camera. "After five years on hiatus, the Race Down Bonebreaker Hill is back! The race was canceled when many riders became lost for days or had their internal organs end up in places they were never meant to go. Natural disasters have also mysteriously dogged its running for several years, capped by the infamous Great Mosquito Swarm of '08. Now, however, with increased security and a new route, we have over a hundred young mountain bikers eager to pit their skills against Bonebreaker Hill." She turned to Erik, who happened to be standing nearby. "Want to tell the audience listening at home your name and how excited you are to be here?" She pushed the microphone into his face.

Erik stared down at the microphone and wondered if he threw up on it what that would sound like to the audience listening at home. After a moment or two of Erik's pale, motionless silence, the television announcer found someone else to chat with.

"Would you like to tell our audience at home about your plans for the race today? What's your name, son?"

"'Sup. Dylan."

Erik put some distance between himself and the

cameras. He was briefly reassured to see an ambulance with EMTs at the start line, but then immediately began to get sweaty. *What could happen at the start line that they'd need an ambulance for?* He started panting in shallow breaths, but noticing this, he was able to switch over to Dragon Breathing and get his body back under control. He stroked his forearm where he had drawn the runes for NO, NEVER, and NOT IN A MILLION YEARS. For the first time, he understood why his sisters and cousins liked sketching rune tattoos on themselves. It was comforting to have words to live by right there on your skin.

The head race official stood up at a podium with a bullhorn and called for attention. "Greetings, racers! If you have not yet picked up your number and registered, please do so. We will begin the race in ten minutes. When the air horn goes off, we'll start the first wave of racers, and this year's Race Down Bonebreaker Hill will begin. We'll be tracking racers' numbers and times on the course to determine our winners in each age group. Emergency personnel are already on the course if they are needed. Let's make it a day to remember! In a good way!"

"Hey, hey, our Hair Shack Hero has arrived!" Coach Gary brought over Erik's paper race number and pinned it to the back of his jersey. He also duct-taped some bear bells to the middle of Erik's handlebars. "You and Fuzz are going to be in the first wave down the hill, so you get to line up in front. They figured if they sent the younger riders down first, the older riders can offer the younger ones help or encouragement if they need it." He looked Erik in the eyes. "Remember that everyone gets nervous about new things, but you've got the training you need to keep out of harm's way. When the air horn blasts, you go for it! I'll see you on the other side."

Erik looked down at his handlebars, relieved when Coach Gary moved on to help Morgan and Leo with their race numbers.

Fuzz arrived with his race number half pinned and half fluttering in the wind. "Sorry I'm late, I almost fell down the stairs, but I then caught myself. Then I jumped up to celebrate so I did fall down the stairs, but I tucked and rolled, so I'm okay," he said. Coach Gary taped on Fuzz's bear bells. "Guess what? Lily asked if she could ride with us, so all three of us can ride together now. We'll be like a constellation of All-Stars!"

Fuzz smiled, and Erik smiled back without having to fake it. Lily joining them was an unplanned bonus — this way, Fuzz really would have a buddy all the way down the hill. What did the Lore say, how life might seem dark but dawn always eventually arrived? It really looked like things were going to work out.

The rest of the Lake Park All-Stars gathered. The older riders clustered together, reviewing the map one last time. The younger girls giggled with Allyson and made up some cheer using the words *bike* and *psych* and *spike*. Dylan had finished his interview with the television crew and was carefully tucking his hair under his helmet and using a tiny mirror to check the effect.

Coach Gary fixed Fuzz's fluttering race number and whistled to get everyone's attention. "Okay, this is it, All-Stars! We've got Lily, Fuzz, and Erik in the first wave, you bunch are in the second and third waves, and Dylan's in the final wave for the oldest riders. You'll mount up, wait for the air horn to blast, and sail out into greatness. Huddle up."

The team came together in a close circle. Fuzz put an arm around Erik's shoulders and grinned at him. Coach Gary stretched out a hand, and each rider added his or her gloved hand atop the pile. Coach Gary chanted, "SLOW and STEADY wins the RACE . . ." pulsing the group of hands up and down along with his words.

The rest of the riders answered back in confident unison, "Let's KEEP our TEETH in our FACE! GOOOOO, ALL-STARS!" and threw their hands up in the air, whooping in excitement. Except for Erik, who squeaked out a sound like "erp," and Dylan, who chanted, "Go, Dylan, go, Dylan, GOOOOO, DYLAN!" Everyone ignored him.

Brunhilde appeared at Coach Gary's side. She cleared her throat to get the cyclists' attention. The team looked at her at little warily, wondering if she would shower them with new nuggets of incomprehensible wisdom. She did not disappoint them.

Brunhilde put one hand over her heart and proclaimed, "None of us live forever. None of us can guess our fates. We can only do our best." She climbed up on a rock and grabbed Leo's bike pump to hold above her head like a sword glinting in the morning sun. "Whatever happens, never give in, never give in, never, never, never, never. As long as there is breath in our bodies, we fight. We yell. We ride!" She brandished the bike pump, and her voice rang out across the crowd. "Now cry havoc! And let slip the bikes of war!"

The mountain bikers were again agape, except for Dylan, who applauded.

"Yeah! Lie in hammocks! And let's grip the highest score!" he said.

Lily climbed up on the rock next to Brunhilde and addressed the team. "I think Brunhilde is saying let's do this and be great!" she said.

Brunhilde lowered the bike pump and shrugged. "Close enough." She climbed off the rock and helped Lily down. Everyone started getting their helmets, kneepads, and elbow pads on for the race.

Each team member's family came over to give last-minute advice and encouragement. The Sheepflattener clan encircled Erik, ready to wish him well. It looked like they had even brought him some presents for the race. He hadn't known this would happen. His neck got hot, but he kept his breathing slow. The time to lie on the ground like a slug and say NO like a Viking would come soon enough.

Allyson recited to him in her best singsong voice, "Ride fast, Erik! You're gonna be epic!" She then squirted something in her hand and wiped it over Erik's face. As he spluttered, she explained, "It's a combination skin bronzer, sunblock, and bug spray? So you look good while you repel mosquitoes and UV rays."

His mother rubbed off some of the excess skin bronzer and told him he looked just like his father before his first boar hunt. Then she showed him her wrist. "See what Allyson did for us!" A flattened sheep looked up at him. The rest of the family showed their wrists too. Allyson had used her colored markers to draw the Sheepflattener crest on everyone.

Allyson pulled out a baby wipe and rubbed Erik's NO, NEVER, and NOT IN A MILLION YEARS runes off his forearm.

"Hey, Allyson, I needed those," he protested.

"Nope, little bro. What you need today is SHEEP-FLATTENER POWER!" She leaned down with a felt-tip pen and started drawing the crossed battle-axes above his wrist.

While his sister sketched, Aunt Hilda and his mother gave him a roll-top pack of sardines and a block of dried turnip to tuck in one of his jersey's three back pockets. Aunt Hilda advised, "Eat those to keep up your energy and don't 'bonk.' I think that's what the kids are calling it these days. We used to call it falling to the inner sabertooth."

His father leaned over the back of his bike frame and secured a small Norwegian flag on a stick with zip ties so it would flutter out behind him as he rode.

Uncle Bjorn pulled a camera out and asked Erik to hold still for a photo "to remember what you once looked like." He got a shot of Ragnar giving Erik a rib-cracking bear hug.

Hrolf sheepishly offered Erik an empty napkin. "I meant to give you the last of this morning's bacon, but I ate it on the way here. The napkin still smells really good, though, if you want a whiff." Erik politely declined.

Brunhilde handed Erik a piece of cloth about the size of a bandanna on which she had outlined a simple version of the Bonebreaker Hill map with a permanent marker. "This will help you stay on track and make sure you don't miss any of your fears on the way down. You can also make a tourniquet out of it if you start to bleed profusely before anyone can get to you." Erik took the cloth and noticed something small and hard tucked inside. He unwrapped the tiny wooden turtle. Brunhilde patted him on the shoulder. "You are ready, Erik Sheepflattener. Do your best. It will be good enough."

His neck got even hotter. As Erik folded the turtle and map into his last empty pocket, Siegmund got his attention by waving his arms. When he was sure Erik was looking, he gave a double baby-thumbs-up. Sally then tugged on Erik's shorts and began making an insistent "uh uh uh" sound. Erik bent down to the stroller to ask what she needed. She solemnly pulled his shirt down and gave him a wet, sticky kiss on his cheek. Erik looked over at Sven. "Do you have something you want to give me too?" he asked.

Sven grinned back, his gums gleaming in the morning sun. He lifted a crumpled brown paper bag out of his lap.

"RIDERS, TAKE YOUR MARKS," the announcer called through his bullhorn.

Fuzz called out, "Erik, come on over, it's time to go!"

"One second, my cousin's got something for me," Erik yelled back. He turned to Sven. "You wrapped it? By yourself?" It was probably a Fanny Fearless book. Erik reached for the bag before it registered in his mind that the bag was moving.

"GET SET."

The top of the bag unfurled like a flower blooming. From the flower's center peeked a familiar pair of glittering black eyes and a whiskery little nose.

Erik shrank away, but Sven wasn't going to let his cousin head out on such an important day without the comfort of a nice soft squirrel ear. Erik might have acted weird the last time he'd been offered one, but he was bound to enjoy it this time. Sven tossed the bag at Erik. It fell with a light thump next to Erik's sneakers.

Mr. Nubbins wriggled free of the brown paper and sat back on his haunches. He reached out his sharp little claws for Erik's shoelace ends, chittering as if to say, *Can I ride along with you? Maybe nibble your skin while you bike? And call the other squirrels over to join in the fun?*

He no longer had it tattooed on his arm, but it was still his motto:

"NOOOOOOOOOOOOOOOOOOOOOOOOOOOOOOOOO
OOOOOOOOOOOOOOOOOOOOOOOOOOOOOOOOOOO
OOOOOOOOOOOOOOOOOOOOOOOOOOOOOOOOOOO
OOOOOOOOOOOOOOOOOOOOOOOOOOOOOOOOOOO
OOOOOOOOOOOOOOOOOOOOOOOOOOOOOOOOOOO
OOOOOOOOOOOOOOOOOOOOOOOOOOOOOOOOOOO
OOOOOOOOOOOOOOOOOOOOOOOOOOOOOOOOOOO
OOOOOOOOOOOOOOOOOOOOOOOOOOOOOOOOOOO
OOOOOOOOOOOOOOOOOOOOOOOOOOOOOOOOOOO
OOO!" screamed Erik right as the air horn blasted to indicate the start of the race.

There was no time for thought, no time for plans, no time to remember how to breathe. Erik leapt onto his bike, stamped on his pedals, and took off from the starting line.

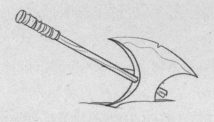

SIXTEEN

MR. NUBBINS VS. DEADMAN'S CLIFF

There are some roads not to follow.
— Sun Tzu, *The Art of War*

Hey, Erik, aren't we going to ride together?" Fuzz exclaimed as Erik blazed by in a flying fury of pedaling legs.

Erik's brain couldn't come up with a sensible answer and instead shrieked, *"Skin nibbler!"* over his shoulder. He cranked his pedals like all the demons of Asgard were chasing him. He plowed over rocks and roots and bumps on the track that he normally would have steered away from. He wasn't considering his path or consciously using any of the techniques he'd practiced with the team. Erik's whole body agreed to work together with one purpose: GO. FAST.

So he went. Fast.

He pedaled and pedaled and pedaled some more. He panted the word *no* until he lost his voice and weak whining *nuh* sounds came out of his throat. No amount of distance seemed safe enough. Mr. Nubbins was so . . . so . . . *squirrelly*. What if he had somehow kept up by leaping behind him from tree to tree? Eventually, Erik got a stitch in his side so painful he had to give his body a break. He squeezed his brakes to a gradual stop. Breath hitching in his throat, he very slowly turned to look over his shoulder.

There was no sign of the Road of Fire portion of the course anymore. He'd already plowed through a big portion of the Rollercoaster Rock Chute and was deep in the forest. He could hear the sounds of other riders' bear bells jingling in the distance, but didn't see anyone — or any*thing* — on the course behind him.

His breath continued hitching in this throat, and his face crumpled in on itself. He sniffed a big wet sniff. He knew he was about twelve seconds away from crying.

He took out his map-tourniquet to wipe his cheeks as a few tears started to mix with the rivulets of sweat. His fast-pumping heart intensified his feelings of the deep unfairness of life and pretty soon his eyes were producing more fluid than his sweat glands. He stood there, side aching, fists clenched around the tourniquet, letting it all drip out.

The bear bell jingle was getting closer. Erik looked back up the trail and saw Lily and Fuzz coming his way. He didn't want them to see him like this, the freaking-out Erik instead of the capable, bike-handling Erik, so he rubbed his face fast with the tourniquet and gulped down some big breaths of air, expanding his belly as Brunhilde was always whapping him on the head to remind him to do. After about five big gulps, the stitch in his side began to fade. He took few slower swigs of air, squishing down his inner turmoil so it wouldn't seem like anything other than normal mountain-biker sweating and flushing.

"Everything okay?" Lily hailed him as she pulled up.

"Dude, you almost cut MY hair, you went by me so fast!" said Fuzz, stopping next to Lily. "I didn't know if we could catch up to you, but here we are. I'm doing super great. I've barely fallen off my bike at all. My mom's never going to believe I found a sport I can actually compete in." He grinned with pride and took a drink of water. "Were you waiting for us? Are you taking a breather before the Deadfall of Doom?"

Erik exhaled slowly. He was not going to retrace his path to the starting line, not with that fast-moving, nut-crunching, tail-twitching creature somewhere back there. He looked around doubtfully. If he faked his stomach upset and lay down now, he might be a sitting duck for Mr. Nubbins. Continuing on to the Deadfall seemed like the only option.

"Taking a breather, right," he answered. "But I think I'm going to walk from here on out." Coach Gary had said he and Fuzz could walk the whole course if things got hairy. Well, things had gotten furry.

"Oh. Okay," Fuzz said. "Should Lily and I stick with you?" He started to dismount, and Erik had to catch Fuzz's arm to steady him when his shoelace caught on his water bottle cage.

Before Erik could answer, Lily tossed her ponytail

over her shoulder and said, "I don't wanna walk, I wanna ride, Fuzz! C'mon! Bye, Erik! We'll save some cookies for you!" She continued rolling down the hill.

"It's fine, Fuzz, I mean, I'm fine," Erik answered. "You go on with Lily. I guess I'm following Coach Gary's rules, you know, slow and steady and keeping my teeth in my face?"

Fuzz said, "You're sure? I don't mind keeping you company." He worked to untangle his shoelace with one hand, clearly struggling to suppress his eagerness to ride on.

"I'm sure. Really. Don't lose our team's head start," Erik said.

"Okay," Fuzz said, relief plain on his face. "See you at Cookies for the Praiseworthy! I'll save you something yummy." His shoelace finally free, he pedaled after Lily.

Erik pushed his Hair Shack Hero bike down the track behind Fuzz and muttered to himself, "Great job, Erik. Now you're going to have to finish this stupid race. Brunhilde couldn't have planned a better exposure therapy nightmare than all this if she'd tried."

Wait a second, a little voice inside of him piped up.

What if she DID plan it? What if she and Sven were working together to create a Squirrel-Infused Explosion of Exposure Therapy? And if she did . . . maybe I just made it through. Maybe I just survived exposure therapy.

The whole idea made him pause. Brunhilde had said exposure therapy meant he'd be forced to confront his phobias until his body and mind got exhausted. Then he'd somehow be cured. He checked his body. It sure felt messed up and exhausted in a lot of ways. His legs were quivering, his throat and lungs still felt raspy.

Am I cured? he wondered. *Fricka's socks, did Brunhilde do it? How can I tell?* He tried to look inside himself to see if his katagelophobia, atychiphobia, enissophobia, or sciurophobia were still in there, but he didn't know if he was doing it right. It felt like he was trying to see the back of his head using two mirrors.

He decided there was no way to know for sure right now. He'd just have to keep walking and see what Brunhilde had to say about all this when he was done with the race.

Erik trudged on, pulling his bike to the side of the

course whenever he heard bear bells behind him. Dozens of racers passed him. Each time a Lake Park All-Stars teammate saw him, they stopped to ask if he needed anything. He reassured them he was playing it safe. He passed an official at the bottom of the Rollercoaster Rock Chute and an EMT in the first part of the Deadfall of Doom.

"All's well, my young friend?" the EMT asked.

"I'm fine, taking it easy," Erik responded for the twentieth time, walking on. He no longer felt like he had to squish down any urge to cry. He also didn't feel scared. Instead, he felt useless. He had practiced right here with his team a few days before. Coach Gary had pointed out how well Erik handled his bike when riding over some roots. Pedaling a bike down Bonebreaker Hill was exciting. Walking a bike down Bonebreaker Hill was not. He dragged his bike over a log, thinking how much easier it was to ride atop two wheels than to lug them along like deadweight.

Maybe I could ride a tiny little bit of the course, the voice in his head piped up again. *To test to see if I cured my phobias with that Exposure Therapy Sprint of Terror?*

That idea didn't motivate him much.

Or mainly because it's fun? He nodded to himself and climbed into the saddle again.

It was a great relief to roll instead of plod through the Deadfall of Doom. Erik completed two bunny hops in a row without a pause for the first time and was pretty pleased with himself as he entered the section Brunhilde had labeled Bears Take the Hindmost. Here, he caught up with several riders who had paused to take a drink of water.

"Howzit?" asked one boy from a group with flower-covered jerseys that said ALOHA. "You from that team that got a chance to practice here? Any advice on getting through this area?"

Erik pulled out his damp map-tourniquet and explained how every rider needed to take it slow with the boulders, keeping their wrists loose. He also pointed out a few narrow pathways to navigate between some large rocks. And he told them how no one should follow the dangerous old trail to Deadman's Cliff and to stay away from the big yellow X of caution tape.

"Thanks, brah," the boy said. "I love this sport. We're all in it together, you know? Us against the elements."

Erik agreed and folded up the map, tucking it back in his pocket. The ALOHA riders headed down the slope and he trailed more slowly behind, following his own advice as vigilantly as possible. He glanced up at the bear caves a couple of times, hoping against hope not to see a brown furry lump making its way down the cliff side. So far, no lumps.

Erik approached one of the trickiest points, where a channel scarcely big enough for a bike to pass through wound between two boulders as tall as his shoulders. He focused intensely on keeping his front wheel straight, looking a scant couple of feet down the trail to scan for obstacles. Once he was almost through, he lifted his eyes to check what the next section of trail had in store.

A gray furry shape poked out from behind a rock.

Erik stopped dead and stopped breathing.

At first, his bear-primed mind yelled, *It's a sniffing*

bear snout! *Bears take the hindmost! That's YOU!* But then the animal hopped into the path, and Erik realized he'd mistaken a little head with black eyes for a snout. He saw its ratty tail. Its missing ear.

Him? How? His lungs deflated, as if he'd had the wind knocked out of him. *How on earth could Mr. Nubbins be HERE? It can't be him. He's far behind. Lots of squirrels must have missing ears, right?* He stared at the squirrel's one good ear and thought he could still see Sven's saliva drying on it. His heart skipped a beat, then made up for it by pounding twice as fast.

A new thought rose up. *Does it actually MATTER whether I'm facing Mr. Nubbins or some other rodent? That animal right there is undoubtedly, completely, tail-twitchingly, one hundred percent SQUIRREL.*

Erik's muscles turned into worthless gelatinous goo. Clammy sweat broke out underneath his exercise sweat. The fear splinters began their internal stabbing. He still hadn't taken a breath since coming upon the squirrel, and his chest began to feel as if an iron band were squeezing it more and more tightly. So, he was wrong, wrong, wrong, wrong, wrong, wrong about exposure therapy curing him. His sciurophobia was alive and well and about to make him pass out.

"'Sup! 'Sup? Move!" shouted a familiar voice right behind him.

Erik choked in a gasp of air. He tilted his head awkwardly and kept his eyes focused on the squirrel as he whispered over his shoulder, "I can't move. There's . . . a . . . problem."

"Yo." Dylan skidded to a stop, bumping Erik's back wheel. "This is, like, no time for sightseeing. Move," he panted.

"I. Can't," whispered Erik. The squirrel twitched his tail, and Erik felt a scream rising in his throat.

"Sure you can. S'easy. Like this," Dylan lifted the back of Erik's bike seat and gave him a mighty shove all the way through the channel only big enough for one bike at a time. Erik was so shocked he lost his grip on his handlebars and grabbed the middle of the headset instead, sliding out of control. He was headed right for the little gray fluffy body. It sat back on its tail and flung open its arms as if to hug him.

Dylan emerged from the channel and passed him

on the left. "See? Gravity's your friend. And you know what Coach Gary always says," the teenager said, nudging Erik hard with his shoulder as he went by. "Win at all costs. Later."

The shoulder nudge sent Erik off-kilter, and he slid to the right, between two boulders, out of sight of the rodent and his teammate. Without those black eyes locked on his, his nervous system unfroze. He managed to get his left hand on the edge of his left handlebar grip and regained a semblance of control. A microscopic feeling of relief pushed its way in among the fear shards choking his body. He was going to be okay. Then Erik saw what was dead ahead.

The big yellow X made of caution tape.

Deadman's Cliff.

He was coming in from an angle where the log blocking the path was not going to stop him. He couldn't get either hand on his brakes in time to stop his forward momentum. *Gravity isn't always my friend!* he had time to think.

Erik and his bike sailed over the edge.

SEVENTEEN

NONE OF US KNOWS OUR FATE

A man that flies from his fear may find that
he has only taken a short cut to meet it.
– J.R.R. Tolkien, an author long believed
to own a secret copy of the Lore

C oach Gary had once told the team that bicyclists
talk about the steepness of hills in different ways.
When a cyclist says, "It's a *good* hill," they can mean
anything from "It's manageable," to "It's really going to
exercise your muscles," to "Anyone who tries riding that
thing is going to meet his maker." In road races, Category 1 climbs are easiest and Category 4 are the hardest,
superseded only by what the French call *Hors Categorie*

climbs or "climbs so unbelievably tough they are beyond categorization, and we don't want to discuss it right now." Erik now found himself in a descent beyond categories. This was not a *good* hill. This was not even a steep hill. This was a near-vertical wall plunging down, down, and more down.

Still pumped up from the fight-or-flight response to Mr. Nubbins — or whoever that squirrel was — his senses were on high alert to danger, so he slipped and slid and swerved and braked like a madman. He aimed his tires toward the sparse grasses clinging to rocky outcroppings to gain any scrap of traction where he could. He found himself reciting rapid-fire, "Don't-wanna-BONK-don't-wanna-BIFF-don't-wanna-BONK-don't-wanna-BIFF!" over and over again.

After balancing and scraping and sliding his way down for about four hours (or four minutes; time didn't really seem to be working exactly right), Erik had almost reached the bottom when his path was blocked by a bike-crunching heap of sharp rocks. He stood on his pedals and leapt sideways, pushing away from his bike and tucking his body into a pill-bug curl. The bicycle crashed among the rocks while he sailed over to land on one shoulder on a flat patch of dirt. He rolled until he stopped rolling, then unfurled on his back and lay in the dirt and stared at the sky for a while.

He took stock of his injuries. Arms and one cheek scraped. Left leg probably bruised. Other leg twitching from exhaustion. Bike? He lifted his head to look. Many haircut stickers missing. One wheel bent in the shape of a taco. Otherwise, he and his bicycle were essentially still in one piece. It was nothing short of a miracle.

"That was nothing short of a miracle!" he heard a distant voice yelling from the top of the cliff.

Erik twisted to look up behind him at what seemed to be an utterly unbikeable block of granite. Way, way, way at the top, he saw the tiny head of a race official.

"Are you okay?" Another head appeared over the cliff, wearing a black and white MEDICAL RESPONSE hat. "Can you hear us?"

Erik pushed himself up into a sitting position and waved. "I'm all right!" he yelled back. "I don't know how, but I am!"

The two small heads turned toward each other and

conferred. "We may have to find some rock climbers to rappel down and rescue you!" called down the first head. "Just stay put!"

"Okay!" Erik shouted. The heads withdrew.

He looked around. What did Brunhilde mean, exactly, when she wrote *Here There Be Dragons*? At the bottom of the cliff was nothing but brushy bushes and cracked piles of old fallen granite. To one side he saw a dense, old-growth forest.

"Here!" the voice above yelled. The man with the MEDICAL RESPONSE hat was lowering a small bag tied to a rope. It took a long time to reach Erik's outstretched hand. He untied and opened the bag and found a bottle of water, an energy bar, a two-way radio, and a piece of paper with a photograph of a cat hanging by its paws to a tree branch with the words HANG IN THERE! printed across the top. The radio crackled into life.

"Can you hear me?" a voice came through. "Just press the yellow button and talk, and then let go when you're done talking."

Erik pressed the yellow button. "I can hear you. I'm okay, but my bike is in bad shape. Isn't there a path somewhere nearby from the last time they did the race, when they used to ride down Deadman's Cliff on purpose? Could you find an old map or something and give me directions on how I can walk out of here? I could carry my bike." He released the button.

"Not a bad idea. What's your name, son?"

"Erik Sheepflattener. I'm with the Lake Park All-Stars. My family is waiting for me at the finish line. Can you tell them I'm fine?"

"Sure thing, Erik. I'm also going to tell them you are one amazing biker. I watched you go over that cliff. I've never seen anything like what you did to get down to the bottom."

Erik looked over his shoulder again. How on earth did he survive that? He guessed he was so focused on getting away from any squirrels that he didn't have the mental energy to waste being scared about anything else. His heart was still hammering and his breath was still coming fast, but it was more of a pumped-up, I-shredded-something-impossible-on-my-bike kind of rush than his familiar I've-gotta-get-out-of-here freak-out.

The radio voice added, "We'll find a way to lead you out of there. Hang tight. Have a snack and rest a bit."

"Thanks." He opened the water bottle and took a long swig. He breathed in. He breathed out. He breathed in. He breathed out. Again, in that almost-against-his-will way it happened when he practiced under the watchful eyes of Brunhilde, he felt his slow breathing begin to soften his belly and loosen up his muscles. He closed his eyes. *In . . . out. In . . . out.* There was no cliff. There were no squirrels. There were no dragons. Only him and his Dragon Breath. In . . . he was a mountain. Out . . . he was a mountain biker. In . . . he was at the bottom of Deadman's Cliff. Out . . . he was not a dead man.

After a few minutes, he opened his eyes. He kept his gaze soft, not really looking for anything. His eyes fell on what looked like an old carving on a sizeable tree at the edge of the dense forest. He went over to examine it. It was a heart with the words *Bill + Quicksand* etched into the bark. Erik rubbed it with one finger.

The radio came to life again in his hand. "Erik, we've got the map. Do you see a path ahead of you?"

Now that he was standing right next to it, he could make out a skinny, barely-there path leading into the trees.

"Sort of," he answered.

"That's the entrance to Quicksand Swamp," the official said. "Do you think you're well enough to walk through there? According to the map, you need to walk about a half mile following that path, and you'll come out right at the meadow almost where the race ends. You should check in by radio every ten minutes or so to let us know how it's going. Think you can do that?"

Erik peered down the path. "I can do it," he said into the radio. He hefted his warped bike over his shoulder. It was either this or wait for a rescue team to come get him, and he didn't really want the attention a rescue team would bring his way. In fact, now he was away from the other racers and the officials and anyone who could criticize or embarrass him. And he was pretty sure Brunhilde hadn't secretly planned any of *this*. There couldn't be anything worse waiting for him ahead than what he'd already survived.

He pressed the yellow button again. "I'm starting in." He began limping into the woods.

"Great! You are some tough kid, I'll tell you that, Erik," the official said. "But remember this—if you see any giant mosquitoes, you drop the bike and run, just RUN. Talk to you in a bit."

EIGHTEEN

ALL'S WELL THAT ENDS

A turnip is best boiled in broth. Yet
whether 'tis boiled, mashed, roasted, or
raw, whether 'tis eaten, or thrown, or forgotten, it remains, ever so, a turnip.
— The Lore

Erik slogged his way through Quicksand Swamp, checking in with the race officials every ten minutes to assure them that he hadn't fallen over any other cliffs, although he did lose his balance once, tumbling with his bike into a smelly puddle of swamp mud. He wiped the glop from his face and felt grateful. Mud puddles were never on his list of scary stuff. The only wildlife he spotted was quite a few rabbits, one deer, and songbirds flittering among the trees, but no bloodsucking insects bugged him.

It took him nearly a half hour, including a short sardine snack break, to get to the finish. He expected the finish line would be deserted, the other racers long since finished and gone home. Instead, there was a throng of people who cheered as soon as Erik emerged from the woods with his bike slung over his shoulder.

His entire family stood together, waving and shouting in Norwegian when they saw him. Allyson was jumping up and down and chanting, "Sheep-flat-ner! Sheep-flat-ner!" Erik waved, and some puddle muck fell off his arm. Hrolf and Aunt Hilda held up the babies, who tossed pinecones in the air and emitted congratulatory streamers of drool. Erik checked Sven's onesie for any sign of wriggling squirrel bits before he let himself get close.

Racers from other teams lifted their cookies and water bottles in salute. As soon as the Lake Park All-Stars saw Erik, they cheered and made whooping noises. All except Dylan, who stood to the side chatting with a news reporter with the winner's ham balanced on his bike's rear rack.

Fuzz shouted, "You made it, Erik! You're the red lantern!"

Erik's father walked over to his son and surveyed his banged-up, scratched-up, mucked-up body. Thorfast grunted. Then he smiled. Then he slapped him on the back with one meaty hand and said in a gravelly voice, "You should be so proud."

The rest of his family came over to towel off some of the mud and congratulate him. Brunhilde took the bike from his shoulder. "I thought you were supposed to ride on this, instead of it riding on you," she said. She pointed at the front wheel. "Why is this part shaped like a hot dog bun? It does not appear to be in the best working order."

"I ended up going over Deadman's Cliff," Erik said.

Ragnar and Hrolf held up their hands to fist-bump Erik, but Brunhilde shouldered them aside and frowned. "What? Was my map not clear?" she said.

"It was Dylan, he came up behind me and pushed

me off the course. I lost control, went over the cliff, and the fall tacoed my wheel." Hrolf snuck back to Erik's side and surreptitiously fist-bumped Erik's scraped-up knuckles. "I'm pretty lucky that was the only thing that turned into a taco."

Allyson looked over at Dylan munching his post-ride cookie and showing off his giant smoked ham to the other teams. Storm clouds began gathering in her face. "Dylan? He did this? *Dylan?*" she said in a dark voice very much unlike her normal bubbling tone. "Excuse me."

Allyson strode toward Dylan. Erik's other teammates and the rest of his family were still trying to clean him up and talk to him about his ride, but Brunhilde dropped Erik's bike and ran after her twin, intercepting her and standing slightly in front of Dylan. Erik watched as Brunhilde started making soothing motions with her hands, perhaps to calm her sister, perhaps to call upon some protective divine forces.

"DYLAN," said Allyson. It was like a Word of Power. The sky darkened, and a rumble of thunder rolled across the treetops. Erik knew she'd officially lost her temper, and it looked like an old god or two were taking notice.

Dylan cocked two fingers at her, clicking his tongue, clueless. "'Sup," he said. "Coming to congratulate me on my win? You can take me out for a milkshake —"

"I cannot stop her," interrupted Brunhilde impatiently. She looked Dylan up and down. "Without a doubt, *you* cannot stop her. You face Allyson Sheepflattener, daughter of Inge and Thorfast, sister of Erik. You would be wise to apologize for what you have done." She nodded her head several times at Dylan.

"Apologize? Stop her? What are you talking about? She's just some girl," Dylan said.

Brunhilde's eyes widened in disbelief. She stopped nodding and stepped back. "I tried to help you, fool. Your fate comes as it comes." She turned to Allyson. "I will go get something to clean up with afterward." She trotted off to the first aid area.

Erik heard Allyson growl, "My little brother said you forced him off the trail during the race. You could have hurt him. Is this true?" It seemed like the air was crackling around her. Other bystanders were unconsciously moving away from Allyson as she spoke.

"You have a brother?" Dylan asked.

Allyson tossed her hair and lightning flashed. "Erik! You know, my brother, Erik Sheepflattener?"

Dylan shook his head and smiled vaguely as if to say, *Never heard of him.*

Allyson said, "You have been practicing with him for weeks. He is on your TEAM. Why would you mess with him?"

Dylan shrugged. "Well, you know, mountain biking is, like, dangerous," he said. "Winning is, like, what it is all about. What can I say? Guess your little brother isn't a winner." He smiled again. "Now, how about that milkshake?"

Dylan continued smiling. Right up until Allyson squeezed her hands around the top tube of his bicycle and snapped the steel in half like a twig.

Erik lost sight of Allyson and Dylan when the group around him shifted and Brunhilde jogged by carrying a couple of towels. When he could see Dylan again, the boy was on the ground and his bicycle had somehow ended up flattened and rolled around him like a tortilla around a burrito.

Allyson stood over him with her hands on her hips, her sundress stained with a few spots of red and pink. Brunhilde raised her eyebrows at the stains and offered Allyson a towel. Allyson waved dismissively and giggled. "Oh, Bru, there's nothing to worry about, it's from the ham."

The skies cleared. Erik watched his sisters walk off arm in arm to get cookies as the paramedics came over to Dylan with a crowbar.

Coach Gary pushed a paper plate full of brownies into Erik's hands. "If anyone deserves a post-ride treat, it is you, my friend. The race officials told me what happened, how you not only survived Deadman's Cliff, but didn't even give up on finishing the race!"

Fuzz jostled through the teammates to give Erik a hug. "I'm glad you're okay. Lily and I feel bad we didn't stick with you."

"Not too bad, though," Lily piped up with a grin. "I

got a prize for Best Rookie Rider." She showed off a mini ham.

Coach Gary said, "Everyone should be really proud of how they did today. Every member of the Lake Park All-Stars crossed the finish line! And no one ended up needing emergency medical assistance!"

Allyson rejoined the group and whispered something in Coach Gary's ear. He said, "Well. Huh. At least nobody ended up needing emergency medical assistance until after the race." He looked over at the paramedics and their crowbar. "I've got to go check on Dylan, so you enjoy the rest of the day with your families. I hope you come back to practice next summer, and bring your friends. Leave your bikes near the cookie table, and I'll make sure they get a tune-up"—here he looked at Erik's bike's taco-shaped wheel—"or whatever, so they're ready for our next ride." He gave them all waves and hugs and headed off.

Hrolf had been standing nearby finishing an oatmeal cookie while pushing the triplets back and forth in their stroller. "Erik! Ma and Da already went home to set up the feasting table. We can head back whenever you want. There will be boar and mushroom pie, and thimbleberry pie, and pike-and-pickerel pie, and fruit-of-the-forest pie."

"That's a lot of pie," Erik answered, mouth full of brownie.

"Ma says feasting is the best way to celebrate family victories and that the Lore says 'Pie for Strength.'" Hrolf licked his lips. "Good job, cousin, giving us a reason for pie." He showed Erik his forearm where he'd added the rough outline of a pie above the Sheepflattener crest. Siegmund, Sven, and Sally clapped their hands.

Erik swallowed and wrinkled his nose. "It wasn't much of a victory, really," he said.

Allyson said, "Are you kidding? You finished the whole race. The whole race! We, like, are soooo impressed. We weren't sure you'd even make it to the starting line or if you'd end up throwing up all over your bicycle first. That's a victory, little bro. For sure."

Ragnar nearly knocked him over by draping his muscled arm over Erik's shoulders. "And you survived a trip over Deadman's Cliff! Not many people, Vikings or otherwise, can say that. When we heard about you going over the cliff and we were waiting to see which bits of you would make it to the finish line, it made some stuff really clear. Really, really clear."

"It did?" Erik asked. "Like what?"

Ragnar nodded decisively. "It's smash. It really is. How could I have thought my rune would be crush?"

"Let's go eat!" Hrolf said.

When the group arrived home, they found that Aunt Hilda and Uncle Bjorn had outdone themselves. The dining room table was barely visible under the array of pies. Uncle Bjorn had placed Brunhilde's red Lego representation of the racecourse as the centerpiece. Ragnar ducked into the kitchen for about ten minutes and came out with a bowl of popcorn. He plunked it down next to Erik with a grin, saying, "I skimped not on the butter and salt."

The family feasted and shared tales of Sheepflattener victories past, from ancient days of yore through Allyson's recent cheer competition. His mother even managed to get Erik to tell the story of how he ended up going over Deadman's Cliff. They roared and grunted their approval when he said, "It was like falling over the edge of the world. Somehow by not thinking about what I was doing, I avoided the things that could have destroyed me and I made it."

Ragnar tossed Sven up toward the ceiling and shouted, "Not thinking gets the job done every time!" Sally clamored to be tossed up next, and soon all three babies were being juggled, much to their delight. Uncle Bjorn started hurling pieces of leftover pie to Hrolf, who caught them in his mouth. Aunt Hilda and Erik's mother sang Norwegian fight songs in two-part harmony. Erik ate another forkful of crust and admitted to himself that the Sheepflatteners did know how to party.

When it was time to clean up, Brunhilde tapped Erik's shoulder and got him to slip outside with her. "We have not yet discussed the success of your phobia battle. I assume it was magnificent. I want to know more details." She had her notebook and pen at the ready.

The solid thing in Erik's gut was with him now, further solidified by all the pie he'd just eaten. He said, "I have to ask you something first. Did you plan with Sven to throw Mr. Nubbins at me at the start of the race? And did you plan with Mr. Nubbins to startle me in the middle of the race?"

Brunhilde regarded him with mild surprise. "No, brother. I did not arrange plans with an infant and a squirrel to help you conquer your worst fears. I am good, but I am not that good."

Relieved his sister didn't have control over everything, he blurted out, "I wasn't going to race. This summer taught me a lot of things, and the stuff we've done has made me sure about my own chosen rune."

Brunhilde put down her pen and looked impressed. "Finding one's rune is serious business, a very personal journey of discovery. Are you ready to share your discovery with me?" she asked.

He decided to go for it. "It's AVOID STUFF."

"Oh, that is silly," she said. "You will have to find something better."

Her dismissal made the solid thing in his guts quiver slightly, but he was on a roll. He summed up what he hadn't had a chance to say at the starting line. "After I refused to race, I was also going to tell you NO and make you listen to me for the first time. I was going to convince you that saying NO is very Viking." He held his breath.

"Saying no IS very Viking," Brunhilde answered. "And I do listen to you. Like right now, I am going to listen to you to tell me about the race after you stop jabbering on about avoiding and saying no to me. Talk," she commanded.

Erik whoofed out a big mouthful of air. *Even if I had thrown up on my bike and collapsed with real stomach cramps, Brunhilde undoubtedly would have tied my feet to the pedals and run alongside me, pushing me down Bonebreaker Hill with her hand on the back of my bike seat.* The solid thing in his guts shrugged. Well, he always knew where he stood with his sister.

He described as much as he could remember of the race, from its fear-fueled start to finding the old path through Quicksand Swamp. Brunhilde took notes. When he was done, she said, "Even after going over the cliff, instead of finding some bed-shaped rock to hide under, you finished the race with your bike on your back." She was scribbling rapidly. "If I understand correctly, sciurophobia may not be your enemy, after all. It may be an odd kind of ally for you. When you see a squirrel, it slams your other phobias out of the way so you can do what must be done." She chewed the top of her glittery pen. "Perhaps we should get our own pet squirrel, and every time you feel like you cannot face something, your other option is squirrel nuzzling. It will put things in perspective for you."

Erik's face drained of blood, and the solid thing in his guts melted into slush. Brunhilde said, "Ha! I am kidding. Here is what you have told me: you came to stand with your teammates to face something you did not want to face. You rode into the mouth of many fears. And you emerged, still whole, still Erik, your shell as thick as ever. We can count this as another Sheepflattener victory." She flipped back to the original page labeled *ERIK VS. FEAR* and made a big check mark at the bottom.

~

The next day, Erik walked over with Hrolf and Ragnar to the Hair Shack. He'd told them he'd be happier skipping the haircut, so they'd offered to use up his free trim in his place. Erik sat near the windows while Hrolf asked the barber to shave a patch over his ear in the shape of a fish and Ragnar had a stylist crimp a couple of skinny black-and-white-striped feather extensions into his hair.

When they got back to show off their new looks, Erik's side of the family had begun packing up to prepare to fly back home to Connecticut. Hrolf kept having to stop the triplets from wiggle-crawling into different suitcases.

"Oh, it's always so wonderful to have the cousins together!" Erik's mother exclaimed. "There's nothing like family. We'd love to host you down in Connecticut soon. Maybe this winter break?" She and Uncle Bjorn and Aunt Hilda compared calendars.

Erik asked Ragnar to accompany him through the house to gather up the last things he needed to pack. "Stay close, in case Mr. Nubbins is hiding somewhere," Erik said as they walked to the bathroom.

"We don't know where he ended up," Ragnar said. "After he scampered behind you down the racecourse, we haven't seen him around."

He DID follow me, Erik thought. *But at least he isn't in the house anymore.* He started to relax, but then tensed up again, realizing that he had no idea when the squirrel might appear again. Was there any way a squirrel could find its way onto an airplane? His mind skittered away from such a question.

"How is Sven taking it?" Erik asked as he picked up his toothbrush and toothpaste. "Does he miss having a wild animal ear to suck on?"

Hrolf walked by the doorway. "Oh, I took care of that this morning. We've got a new pet."

Erik poked his head out of the bathroom to ask where his cousin had found a new pet so quickly, and a blur of light brown fur shot by with a Sven-shaped blur holding on to its back.

"What the—"

The blur of fur let out a high-pitched yowl, and Siegmund and Sally followed behind, wiggle-crawling at top speed and howling in response.

"You have a BOBCAT as your pet now?" Erik said. "That's crazy!"

"It's only a baby bobcat. We'll build him a cat door so he can come and go as he pleases," Ragnar said. "Mom said it was okay."

The young cub lost control of its wide fluffy paws and slid into a wall at the end of the hall. The triplets caught up to it and snuggled next to it in a pig-pile . . . or cat-pile, as the case may be. The bobcat's tongue curled out as it gave a mighty, toothy yawn. The babies yawned too, each showing a single sharp tooth of their own. Sven plugged one of the cub's ears in his mouth and began sucking happily. He noticed Erik watching him in horrified disbelief and waved bye-bye.

It was time to go home.

~

On the way to the airport, Erik and Brunhilde had one last stop to make. They entered the children's section of the library to return *Fanny Fearless Fries a Fish, The Big Book of Fear,* and the regular and the toddler versions of *The Art of War* to Mrs. Harkness.

Brunhilde bowed on one knee and raised the books over her head. "Thank you for lending us these tomes of knowledge. And the Fanny Fearless books. She is quite the character."

Mrs. Harkness smiled. "You can drop them in the returns slot. I hope you found *The Big Book of Fear* especially helpful. Did you know I used to have a phobia myself? It's called bibliophobia."

Brunhilde quickly paged through the *B* section. She looked up, brow creased. "The fear of books?"

Mrs. Harkness winked. "Exposure therapy can do wonders, my dears. One has to stick with it, though. I personally found that a single treatment was not enough — only extreme measures worked in my case."

Brunhilde looked thoughtfully at Erik, who immediately began shaking his head. "Nope, Bru, no, no, no," he said. "Your measures were extreme enough. We're counting my race as a victory, don't you remember, and doesn't Sun Tzu say *There are some roads not to follow, some troops not to strike . . . ?*"

They walked out of the library, Erik still trying to make a convincing argument, and Brunhilde pulling out her glittery pen.

NINETEEN

THE WALNUT RIDES ON

One must howl with the wolves one is among.
— The Lore

Unpacking his suitcase at home, Erik was missing something he'd begun working on during the plane ride. He walked over to his sisters' room to see if one of them might have seen it. He knocked on the door frame to get Brunhilde's attention and saw his new red notebook in her hands.

"That's mine. Can I have it back?" he asked.

Brunhilde ignored him, flipping through the first few pages of Erik's notebook, the same size and style as her own purple one. She read the headings out loud: "ERIK

VS. MOM SIGNING ME UP FOR ACTIVITIES, ERIK VS. THE TEACHER CALLING ON ME IN CLASS, ERIK VS. MR. NUBBINS EVER FINDING ME AGAIN." She grunted in amusement at her little brother's attempts to plan combat strategy.

"That's private? I'd like it back now?" Erik said. He tried to make his voice firm, but his voice insisted this was a good time to speak in nervous questions instead.

Brunhilde kept ignoring him and continued to flip through the mostly unused notebook. She stopped flipping to look at a heading labeled *ERIK + MOUNTAIN BIKING*. Written underneath was the rune for UNCONQUERABLE. The opposite page had originally been titled *ERIK VS. BRUNHILDE MAKING ME DO STUFF*, but he'd scratched out replaced part of it , so the new title was *ERIK + BRUNHILDE HELPING ME DO STUFF*.

Erik took one step across the threshold. If Brunhilde went into her battle stance, he would give up on the notebook and get himself a new one.

Brunhilde looked up, her eyes unreadable. She snapped the notebook closed. "I believe this belongs to you, brother," she said.

Erik snatched the notebook and scuttled back to his own room.

~

Weeks later, Mrs. Sheepflattener called out using her I-know-you-can-hear-me-from-half-a-block-away voice, "Children! Food's ready! Why isn't the table set yet?"

Brunhilde and Allyson came in from working with the horses, and Erik joined them in the dining room. One sister handled silverware, the other plates, and Erik took care of napkins and mugs. The table was ready before their parents sat down in their chairs with contented sighs.

"Mom, Mom, Mom, I have news!" Allyson squealed as she took her seat. "Bobby Tamboris came by cheer practice today and asked if I'd go with him to the homecoming dance! Bobby TAMBORIS!"

Their mother said, "Isn't he one of the boys who work part-time at the feed store? Strong back on that one. Can lift hay bales without a whimper. Seems like a fine choice for a dance partner."

Brunhilde snorted. "Bobby Tamboris," she said. "I

suppose he is better than that Dylan character from this summer."

Allyson tossed her hair and smiled. "Oh, Bru, don't be jealous. I'm sure one of Bobby's friends would take you to the dance if I asked him."

"Please do not," Brunhilde said.

"What if I *insisted* one of his friends bring you?" Allyson clasped her hands together and flexed her biceps.

Brunhilde met her sister's eyes. Erik moved his mug out of the way, waiting to see if she'd go for her battle-axe. Instead, Brunhilde said, "Ha! I would like to see any boy withstand the insisting of Allyson Sheepflattener. But I have no time for dancing. Debate team tryouts are next week."

Erik's mother said, "Tryouts, that reminds me! Erik, did you go to any of the club tryouts after school?"

"Mom, no," he moaned.

Allyson looked his way. "Which phobia is it that's keeping you from the tryouts, Erik? Enissophobia? Atychiphobia? Do you need me to come to the elementary school and do some insisting they let you in?" She flexed her biceps again and showed a new rune. This one said SISTER.

Brunhilde punched one fist into her other hand and asked, "Tell them if they need an assistant coach, I could be available. It seems I am quite good at coaching groups."

Erik put his face in his hands.

Mrs. Sheepflattener said briskly, "Erik, since you're not going to be doing piano lessons, you have to find something else to fill your time. Kids must stay busy, Odin knows."

"I'm not doing piano lessons?" Erik looked up.

"Not anymore. Brunhilde came to me and asserted that she needs your piano time for her own training. She said you didn't appreciate what Mrs. Loathcraft could teach you, while she could." Their mother shrugged. "You certainly strain my muscles dragging you in there in each week, so I said yes."

Erik opened up his mouth, found he didn't know what to say, and shut it again. Brunhilde leaned toward him and said quietly, "I thought you could find something else to do after school if you did not have piano lessons to face. Something more fun for you. Maybe something involving two wheels?"

Erik still didn't know what to say. He took in a deep breath and let it out slowly. Then he did it one more time. *In . . . my sister is rescuing me from piano lessons. Out . . . why? In . . . my sister. Out . . . rescuing me.*

The phone rang. Technically, it yelled "gaaah!" rather than rang. In Erik's voice. He let out a confused little *eeep* as his mother got up to answer it.

"Oh yeah, like what I did with mom's phone?" asked Allyson. "I programmed her ringtone as your phone-yelp."

"You recorded me?" Erik said. "Why?"

"I figured it would save us time, since we usually wait for you to yell after the phone rings so we're all sure it rang. Great idea, right?" She took another heaping forkful of fish chunks.

"As long as no one decides to grab the phone and punch it, I guess it's okay," Erik said, thinking of Ragnar.

Their mother came back into the room, face bright. "That was your father's cousin Sif calling from Miami— they're planning a family reunion this winter! They said they've been taking lessons in something called salsa dancing and they want to teach us the moves. Apparently, they're as good for the core muscles as the Sheepflattener Stomp-Round from the Lore."

Allyson said, "Wow, I want to learn that. When are we going?"

Talk turned to what to pack for a winter trip to Miami. The discussion of Erik's keeping busy was momentarily forgotten.

~

Brunhilde's fingers drummed on her leg with the relentless beat of a military march. Her mother sat next to her, reading a romance novel.

The door marked STUDIO #3 opened.

A girl with her hair wrapped up in tiny braids walked out of the studio. "Remember to use the metronome every time you practice, Denise," said Mrs. Loathcraft, waving goodbye. She saw Brunhilde sitting next to Mrs. Sheepflattener, and her face creased into a frown. "Where is Erik?" she asked.

Brunhilde stood and offered her hand. "I am Brunhilde Sheepflattener, sister of Erik." Mrs. Loathcraft took her hand and shook it cautiously. "I will be taking lessons with you now instead of Erik. He no longer has room in his schedule for your teachings."

"Hmmph," said Mrs. Loathcraft. "Do you have any previous musical experience?"

"I like to listen to Wagner's 'Ride of the Valkyries' when I practice hand-to-hand combat. Otherwise, no. But I have not come here to learn piano."

Mrs. Loathcraft leaned back against the door frame and folded her arms. "Why are you here, then? What do you think I can teach you if not piano?" she asked.

Brunhilde said, "Erik speaks of you in such terrifying terms. He believes you have the power to wither a student's confidence with one glance, to turn their insides to a quivering mass of icy gel with a single word. I have come to try and learn your ways. This would be invaluable for field hockey games, not to mention debate team tryouts. Are you willing to share your secrets of crushing those who dare to stand before you?"

Mrs. Loathcraft glanced around to see if anyone else was paying attention to their conversation. None of the other parents or children appeared to have overheard. She leaned in closer to Brunhilde and clasped her elbow.

"Come inside, young lady." The piano teacher's face gave Brunhilde a happy shiver of anticipation. "I think you have come to the right place."

"Have fun!" her mother said, waving as the door shut behind them.

Forty-five minutes later, the weekly lesson was over. It is safe to say that not everyone would describe the lesson as fun. However, it is also safe to say that fun was, most assuredly, had. Brunhilde gripped Mrs. Loathcraft's hand in both of hers before heading out.

"See you next week, teacher," she said.

~

The first day of fall, Spjut the terrier was waiting patiently when the school bus pulled up from Ridgewell Lower Middle School. He sniffed each child as they disembarked and gave most of them a tail wag. Erik was the last one off, running immediately for his yard, Spjut at his heels. The front door banged shut behind them. Erik headed up the stairs. The dog followed, his tiny toenails clicking on the wooden stair risers. He arrived in time to see Erik slide under his bed as usual.

Spjut turned in a circle three times on Erik's braided rug, about to settle in for his afternoon nap, but startled into full wakefulness when Erik slithered back out from under the bed, pulling his new bike helmet with him.

"Want to come along, Spjut?" Erik asked him. "We're meeting today over at the Peaked Mountain trailhead. You have to promise not to bark at any of the bikes, though, okay?"

Spjut's tongue dangled in cheerful anticipation. He had heard the words *bark* and *bikes*. Sounded like his kind of afternoon.

He followed Erik to the garage, where the boy rolled out his secondhand mountain bike. It was not as nice as the bike he'd used this summer, but it would do. He couldn't beat the price, that was for sure. Every hour he put in cleaning up at the local bike shop was put toward the value of the bike. Once he'd worked one hundred hours, the bike would be his.

The day after he'd learned he didn't have to take any more piano lessons, Erik had summoned up that solid thing in his guts and asked the school secretary for a list of the after-school groups that involved bicycles. Two were listed: the Ridgewell RaceWell Cyclonauts and the Ridgewell RideWell Mountain Bike Club. Erik knew he didn't want anything to do with racing, so he'd gone to the first meeting of the RideWell Mountain Bike Club in the grease-scented back room of the bike shop. Jorge, a high school senior, was the club leader.

"Welcome, bikers," Jorge said. "First off, I want you to know this is a club, not a team, and we don't race like the maniacs over in the Cyclonauts do. If competition's your thing, you are in the wrong place, so feel free to leave if you want, no hard feelings." He gazed around the room. No one got up to leave. "Fine and dandy, guess we're here all here to learn some skills and enjoy the outdoors. Now, anyone here done this before?"

A few other kids raised their hands. Erik started doing Dragon Breathing to keep from hiding under the workbench or snack table and raised one finger.

Jorge said, "Right. Let's pretend we're all beginners and start with some basics. If you didn't bring your own bike, grab one that fits you off that rack over there, and let's head outside."

The group started off by reviewing some safety point-
ers and then did a very short ride down the block and
around an empty soccer field. Erik didn't say a word,
rode at the back, and tried to stay out of the way. He did
the same at the next meeting, and the next. But he kept
showing up. His riding skills still weren't much to speak
of, but he did brilliant tuck-and-rolls whenever he fell
off his bike. After a few rides together, the other members of club voted unanimously to nickname Erik "the
Walnut" for his well-protected biking style. He liked it.

He and Spjut pedaled up for the day's ride with his
fellow RideWell club members. He hadn't told his family
about the club yet. He wanted to be sure Brunhilde and
Allyson wouldn't decide to "help" him with his practices
and his mother wouldn't decide that if joining one bicy-
cling club was good, joining two, or three, or five would
be even better. The Walnut was going to keep this one
under his shell for as long as he could.

Maybe, once he'd gone on a few more rides with the
club, he'd tell his sisters about it, if they wanted to know
what he was up to. Maybe he'd even invite them to come
try riding with him. He pictured Allyson giggling on a

pink bike and sailing over giant boulders, and Brunhilde encouraging everyone to learn an Old Norse battle cry, waving her CONQUEST rune at the head of the pack. Maybe his mom and dad would even want to come along on a couple of their horses. At the end, maybe they could ride somewhere together for pie and talk about Sheepflattener family victories.

Erik pulled down his sleeves to cover the symbols he'd scrawled on his own forearms that morning. The right one said AVOID MOST STUFF. The left one was the Sheepflattener family crest. He was still pretty sure his family didn't know the meaning of the word *fear*. Or the word *no* — at least when he said it. But he thought they all might agree on the meaning of the word *family*.

"Hey, Walnut, you coming? Time to head out," called Jorge as he led the pack into the woods.

"Coming!" Erik brought up the rear. Behind and above him, leaves shook in the canopy of the oak trees. One tiny, tattered squirrel ear had swiveled toward the bikers at the mention of the word *Walnut*. Now the squirrel was following the group, making sure not to be seen while leaping from branching to branch, keeping Erik in his line of sight.

Luckily, Erik was too caught up in pedaling to notice. For now, there were mountains to be biked.

THE END

ERIK VS. EVERYTHING:
SOURCES FOR QUOTATIONS

It turns out that bits of the Sheepflattener Lore as well as some of Erik's screams and Brunhilde's advice come from a variety of books and famous people. The Sheepflatteners and I are indebted to the following:

"One must howl with the wolves one is among" is a proverb that has been translated from the Danish a few different ways, but this one is my favorite. You'll find it and others at the *Viking Rune* website (www .vikingrune.com/2012/12/norse-proverbs-and-sayings). "That which is hidden in the snow turns up in the thaw" is a proverb that can be found in *The Neigh-bours, A Story of Everyday Life,* by Frederika Bremer;

translated from the Swedish by Mary Howitt. London: Henry G. Bohn, 1852.

Whenever Erik's screams are one hundred letters long or more, he's unconsciously quoting made-up words from author James Joyce's book *Finnegan's Wake*.

Chapter Nine's breathing instructions are based on the teachings of Buddhist monk Thich Nhat Hanh. He's written many books about meditation and mindfulness; *A Handful of Quiet: Happiness in Four Pebbles* is a great one for kids.

Frank Herbert's book *Dune* inspired the cheer beginning "We will face our fear." The real quote is "I will face my fear. I will permit it to pass over me and through me. And when it has gone past I will turn the inner eye to see its path. Where the fear has gone there will be nothing. Only I will remain."

Brunhilde really likes Winston Churchill's speeches. Her encouragement to the cyclists to "never give in, never give in, never, never, never, never" is something Churchill said in 1941, and her speech beginning "We shall not flag or fail. We shall go on to the end . . ." is a mutilated version of a famous speech Churchill gave to Parliament in 1940. She's also fond of Shakespeare. When she says, "Lend me your ears," and then later shouts, ". . . cry havoc! And let slip the bikes of war," she's quoting from his play *Julius Caesar* (although in his version, it's "the dogs of war").

All quotes from Sun Tzu's *The Art of War* come from the beautifully illustrated 2016 edition of this work published by Arcturus Publishing Limited, London, which uses the Samuel Griffith translation.

"A man that flies from his fear may find that he has only taken a short cut to meet it" was said by a character in *Unfinished Tales of Númenor and Middle-earth*, a collection of stories by J.R.R. Tolkien never completed during his lifetime, but edited and published by his son Christopher Tolkien in 1980.

AN ANXIOUS AUTHOR'S NOTE

As the veteran of one tour of an anxious childhood, I know that fears, anxieties, and phobias are no joke. The problems against which Erik battles are real for many children and adults. The good news is that there is help even for those of us without Viking families.

If you have trouble with worries or anxiety, please take the first step of talking to a teacher, counselor, friend, or family member about what is going on. Many useful treatments offer proven ways to help train your body and mind to calm down, including relaxation techniques like deep breathing, meditation, and Mindfulness-Based Stress Reduction. (I can assure you that absolutely no one recommends being locked in a cage with a ringing phone and a squirrel.)

Lots of doctors and therapists understand what you are going through, not to mention many other grown-ups like me. You are not alone. As Brunhilde would say, "We will always be on your side and vanquish that which would trouble you."

ACKNOWLEDGMENTS

May the old gods shower countless blessings upon the following people who helped me with Erik's story and beyond:

My team at HMH and my lovely editor, Lily Kessinger, who understood right off the bat that Erik was ME and pointed out the weird things that made her laugh.

My agent, Ammi-Joan Paquette, and the gang of talented, generous, and kind people who make up the Erin Murphy Literary Agency.

My family, who are always on my side and would vanquish that which would trouble me. Jack and Susannah, thanks for treating Brunhilde and the crew like they're our actual relatives. Also, my parents deserve special thanks for letting me say NO to many, many things when I was young so I could simply stay in my room and read.

My friends, who remind me of the things to which I enjoy saying YES, like all-day breakfast restaurants.

My home libraries of East Longmeadow and Longmeadow, and all the wonderful libraries and classrooms around the country that have invited me to visit and connect with readers.

I'm so grateful that you are the wolves among whom I get to howl, the warrior figurines surrounding my walnut, the butter and salt on the popcorn of my life.